"Marriage Is W̶̶̶̶̶̶̶̶̶ Aiming For, ̶̶̶̶̶̶̶̶̶ It.̶̶̶"

She quickly shook her head. "No! I didn't. I—"

"Enough lying. You're trying to get someone to marry you and you'll use any means—any *person*—to keep your son." His lips twisted. "I guess I'm just damn lucky I was the one on hand."

"No! I have no intention of marrying you—or anyone else, for that matter. I've just lost my husband, for God's sake," she said, her voice catching.

"That didn't stop you sleeping with me last night, did it?"

She sucked in a breath. "That was a mistake. We've already agreed not to repeat it."

"I told you before I don't like being used."

"I'm sorry. If I could take it back without harming my son, then I would."

A nerve pulsed near his temple. "Fine. I'll be your fiancé for now. But I can tell you this, Vanessa. I will *never* be your husband."

Dear Reader,

When my editor suggested I write an Outback story for the BILLIONAIRES AND BABIES series along with two other wonderful Australian Silhouette Desire authors, Robyn Grady and Paula Roe, I was thrilled. Not only do I love writing characters drawn together for the sake of a child, but who wouldn't want to write a story set in the romantic Outback? It's a special place that deserves a special love story.

The term *Outback* is not a precise location, and even Australians don't know exactly where the Outback starts and ends. Many Australians live in the cities, others in rural areas called "the bush," and farther out—somewhere "out back"—it turns into the "Outback." Where the line is drawn no one really knows. You're suddenly there in the middle of something that entrances a person in a way you've never known before and you just know that this is it. It's a bit like love.

Of course, Vanessa Hamilton and Kirk Deverill aren't quite so quick to realize they have a love like no other. Vanessa has been mourning her late husband and is now busy trying to protect her son from his smothering grandparents. Kirk has a secret he won't burden any woman with. There are just too many reasons for them not to fall in love.

And if that's the case, then perhaps they'll manage to escape the romantic lure of the Outback. Then again... perhaps they won't. I hope you enjoy this story.

Happy reading!

Maxine

MAXINE SULLIVAN

HIS RING,
HER BABY

Silhouette®

Desire

Published by Silhouette Books
America's Publisher of Contemporary Romance

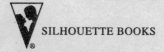

SILHOUETTE BOOKS

Recycling programs
for this product may
not exist in your area.

ISBN-13: 978-0-373-73021-6

HIS RING, HER BABY

Visit Silhouette Books at www.eHarlequin.com

Printed in U.S.A.

Books by Maxine Sullivan

Silhouette Desire

*The Millionaire's Seductive Revenge #1782
*The Tycoon's Blackmailed Mistress #1800
*The Executive's Vengeful Seduction #1818
Mistress & a Million Dollars #1855
The CEO Takes a Wife #1883
The C.O.O. Must Marry #1926
Valente's Baby #1949
His Ring, Her Baby #2008

*Australian Millionaires

MAXINE SULLIVAN

credits her mother for her lifelong love of romance novels, so it was a natural extension for Maxine to want to write her own romances. She thinks there's nothing better than being a writer and is thrilled to be one of the few Australians to write for the Silhouette Desire line.

Maxine lives in Melbourne, Australia, but over the years has traveled to New Zealand, the U.K. and the U.S.A. In her own backyard, her husband's job ensured they saw the diversity of the countryside, from the tropics to the Outback, country towns to the cities. She is married to Geoff, who has proven his hero status many times over the years. They have two handsome sons and an assortment of much-loved, previously abandoned animals.

Maxine would love to hear from you. She can be contacted through her Web site at www.maxinesullivan.com.

To my fabulous agent, Jennifer Schober.
Thanks for your support and enthusiasm, Jenn.

And to Catherine Evans for her helpful advice
with the Outback scenes. Thanks, Cath.

One

We've sold the motel.

Vanessa Hamilton was still reeling from her cousin's news when she looked up and saw a luxury Range Rover pull up out front of the Jackaroo Plains Motel.

She groaned, wishing she could go think about her situation without interruption from either telephones or guests. Her son was taking his morning nap right now so the timing would have been perfect. She was pleased for Linda and Hugh, of course. It was what they wanted. But she'd only been here three weeks and had planned on staying at least six months.

And right now she had to put all her worry aside as she watched the man push open the glass door. Lord, he was certainly handsome enough to take any woman's mind off her problems.

Or *create* one.

No one had taught her about these three Rs in school.

Rich.

Rugged.

Red-blooded.

He epitomized everything she imagined a wealthy outback male to be. From the tips of his brown leather boots, to bone-colored trousers and the light blue polo shirt a woman was tempted to rub against, to his wrist where an expensive Rolex glistened in the light.

He stopped in front of the reception desk, his blue eyes filling with masculine appreciation. "You're new here," he drawled.

She lifted her chin, annoyed with herself for finding him attractive. "Are you looking for a room?" she asked in her best no-nonsense voice, already knowing they had nothing suitable. The Plaza Hotel in New York was more his style.

Those blue eyes narrowed on her. "No."

"If you're looking to eat in the restaurant—"

"I'm not."

"You're not here for the gardener's job, are you?" she said, knowing it sounded ridiculous but one never knew.

His low chuckle resonated with something inside her. Something she didn't want to acknowledge.

"No, I'm not here for that, either."

Suddenly she noticed his gaze dart to her left hand, noting her bare fingers. Uneasiness fluttered inside her stomach that he might think her single and available. It had been weird taking off her rings, but the heat had made her fingers swell a little and the alternative had been to have the rings adjusted. She hadn't wanted to do that, seeing her fingers would return to normal once she returned to Sydney.

Just like *she* would return to normal, she had promised herself, realizing now it might happen sooner than expected.

Oh, God, she didn't want to go back to the city where her wealthy parents-in-law doted on her one-year-old son, Josh.

More than doted.

Smothered.

"I came to see Linda and Hugh," the man said, drawing her back to the present.

The penny dropped. He was the new owner of the motel. Oh, yes, that explained him. Her cousin said he was rich, predatory, and sucked up failing businesses like a vacuum cleaner, then got rid of half the staff under the guise of modernization.

Well, officially *she* wasn't on the staff.

She gave him a cool look. "They're not here."

"Where are they?"

"Dubbo."

There was a moment's pause. "When will they be back?"

"No idea."

One brow lifted, a questioning light in his eyes. "Are you always this helpful?"

"Only when it's part of the job," she said with a politeness that was nothing more than lip service.

His jaw set. "Look, I'm a friend of Linda and Hugh's and—"

Her heart thudded. "A…a friend?"

"Yes, Hugh and I went to boarding school together."

"Oh, I thought—" She stopped. Perhaps Linda and Hugh didn't want it known yet that they were selling.

"Yes?"

"It doesn't matter." It all made sense now. She could easily see the two men being friends. Hugh's parents owned a cattle station, but Hugh had been more interested in business than the land and had bought the motel for him and Linda.

Did this man own a cattle station, too? He certainly looked like one of the wealthy landowners.

"The name's Kirk, by the way," he said, snapping her from her thoughts. "Kirk Deverill."

His name flowed over her. Why couldn't he be called Bruce? Or Darryl? Something that didn't sound so masculine or make a woman think about him as a man.

She let out a shaky breath. "I'm Linda's cousin. Vanessa Hamilton."

He paused, as if putting the name to her face and liking what he saw. Then his eyes fell to her lips. "I didn't know Linda had such a beautiful cousin."

She gave a soft gasp. Why did this man's words make her knees weak when almost every available male in town, and some not so available, had said the same thing since her arrival?

The telephone rang and she snatched it up, uncomfortable at the feelings he was raising inside her. She could feel him watching her as she went to a stand to get a brochure on the Western Plains Zoo at Dubbo. She answered a couple of questions for the guest then hung up and put the brochure back.

"I'm sorry. I—" She looked up and caught him eyeing the full length of her denim jeans. "Um…just a question about the zoo," she finished on a lame note.

"No need to be sorry," he said smoothly, not looking the slightest bit uncomfortable at having been caught. Then he considered her. "So tell me. Why the attitude?"

She cleared her throat. "Attitude?"

"You obviously thought I was someone else."

"Perhaps." It wasn't up to her to tell him about the sale. Besides, he could say he was a friend of Linda and Hugh's but that didn't mean he actually was.

"Someone you don't like."

"Maybe."

"You realize you owe me an apology," he pointed out.

Yes, and he owed her an apology for the way he'd been looking at her, but did she want to go there? No way.

"Of course, there is a way you could make up for it," he said, a light in his eyes telling her this man was very experienced with women.

She stiffened. *Here it comes.* One sexist remark and she'd tie him to a tree for the dingoes to eat.

"Have dinner with me tomorrow night."

"Dinner?" Her heart jumped in her chest. "I can't. I mean, I can't desert Linda and Hugh then. It's going to be a big night for them. I'm helping out around the place, you see, and I—"

"You only had to say no." Her reaction seemed to amuse him. "I'm a big boy. I can take it."

Vanessa didn't know whether to be relieved or irritated that he gave in so easily. She'd expected some sort of fight from the guy.

She drew breath. "Fine then. No, I don't want to have dinner with you tomorrow night."

"How about a rain check?"

She gave a startled laugh. "What happened to 'you only had to say no'?"

"I said I could take it. I didn't say I would." An air of indolence exuded from him. "Now, about that rain check…"

All at once she wanted to get the better of him. "Okay," she said, planting a smirk on her lips. "Next time it rains I'll have dinner with you."

His brow rose. "You realize we're in the middle of a severe drought, don't you?"

"Yes, I know."

His firm lips relaxed into a lazy smile and her stomach did a flip-flop. Suddenly she wanted to step around the counter and into his arms. Arms that would snake around her hips and pull her up against his aroused body.

Aroused? Yes, she had the feeling she could excite this man, if she chose to make a move on him.

Not that she would, she told herself as she mentally pulled away in confusion. She'd never felt such an instant reaction before. With Mike the attraction had grown as she'd slowly fallen in love.

Mike.

Oh, God, how could she even think about comparing her late husband to this stranger? What was wrong with her today? Maybe it was just too much stress. In any case, it was definitely too much of—

"Kirk!" Linda exclaimed, coming through a side door with Hugh, sending a sigh of relief through Vanessa, who was more than ready to go clean some of the vacated rooms. "You're back from Sydney at last."

"Yes, just passing through on the way home." He gave Linda a kiss on the cheek and shook Hugh's hand. Then his gaze slid across the reception desk. "Your cousin's been looking after me."

Linda darted a smile at Vanessa. "Good."

"Did she tell you about the sale?" Hugh said.

Kirk brows drew together. "Sale?"

Vanessa gave Hugh a helpless smile. "I wasn't sure if I should say anything."

"That's okay, love," Hugh said warmly. "Kirk, we put the motel on the market a few weeks ago and this morning we received our first reasonable offer. That's why we rushed into Dubbo. To sign the contract."

A frown crossed Kirk's face. "You're selling?"

"It's either sell now or lose everything," Hugh said, then his face brightened. "But I've been offered a job to manage some apartments on the Gold Coast. It's come at the perfect time. Linda and I want to have another baby in the not-too-distant future." He hugged his wife to his side. "Don't we, darling?"

Linda smiled up at him. "A little brother or sister for Toby would be lovely."

Kirk scowled. "Listen, if you need money to keep the motel afloat—"

Hugh shook his head. "Thanks, mate, but it's been getting too much for us anyway. It'll be nice to have a normal family life again."

Vanessa watched Kirk seriously consider his friends, then give a slow nod. "I'll be sorry to see you both go."

"Hey, we'll only be a few hours away by air," Linda said.

"When does the sale go through?"

"We're handing over in a month's time." Hugh grimaced. "The buyer is Bert Viner and you know what his reputation is like. I don't like selling to him but—" He put up his hand as Kirk went to speak. "No, we're fine, Kirk. It's time for us to move on."

Linda sighed. "Unfortunately he'll cut back on staff and I hate that people will lose their jobs. And Vanessa was going to stay for six months but now…" Linda looked at her cousin and her eyes clouded over. "I just didn't think it would happen this quickly."

Neither had she, Vanessa thought, forcing a smile. "Oh, Linda, it's not like you hadn't told me that you'd put the motel on the market."

"I know but—"

"Don't worry about me. This is your *life* we're talking about." They'd worked hard to get to this point in their lives.

"I know but—"

"I've had a nice break," Vanessa said firmly.

Linda took a shuddering breath, then her face filled with resolve. "You're my cousin. We'll think of something."

Vanessa's heart softened as she looked at Linda's upset face and Hugh's concerned one. These two people had welcomed her into their home with love and affection and she didn't want them to feel guilty about any of this.

Then she realized Kirk's intense gaze was on her. He couldn't know her circumstances but she suspected he knew she was deeply worried.

So she welcomed Linda's exclamation. "Oh, heavens, Kirk! We're standing here talking to you instead of offering you a drink. Or how about I make you some lunch? The restaurant's closed but I'd be happy to whip something up for you."

Kirk's smile said thanks but he replied, "Sorry, I can't. I need to get home and do some catching up. I've been away too long."

Linda's expression turned sympathetic. "I'd heard your housekeeper had to go interstate to take care of a family member. It won't be easy getting someone to replace her." She pulled a face. "And here, I haven't even asked how your mother is after her surgery. There were some complications, I believe."

"Yes, but she's finally on the mend. Jade's looking after her now, when she's not working all the hours under the sun, that is."

"I wonder who your sister is like?" Linda teased, then her eyes widened. "Oh, I almost forgot. It's Hugh's parents' thirty-fifth wedding anniversary tomorrow and we're giving them a party in the restaurant. You must come, Kirk. They'd be heartbroken if you didn't. Isn't that right, Hugh?"

"You know they always had a soft spot for you," Hugh said, going over to one of their guests who'd come in and made a beeline for the brochure stand.

"I don't see how," Kirk joked after him, and Vanessa had

to wonder the same thing, too. The man had a hardness about him that didn't translate into him being more a friend than a foe. Yet watching him here with Linda and Kirk—and he evidently treated his mother and sister well—didn't fit. That hardness was more than skin deep, she was sure.

"I'll see what I can do," he added.

"Good," Linda said, taking that for his word. "And if you don't mind, you can keep an eye on Vanessa. She doesn't know many people in Jackaroo Plains. She's only been here from Sydney three weeks."

Vanessa froze.

"It would be my pleasure," she heard Kirk say.

She recovered quickly. Her cousin was a mother hen at times but *she* didn't need looking after, and certainly not by a man who dined on women for breakfast.

"I'll be fine, Linda. I don't want to take Kirk away from the other guests."

"You won't," he said, a purposeful gleam in his eyes sending a shock through her, though it shouldn't have. He'd been making a move on her since he'd walked through the door, and mentally she was already *his*.

"There you are then," Linda said, giving Vanessa an encouraging smile. All at once she tilted her head thoughtfully. "You're looking quite flushed, sweetie. It's this outback heat. You haven't got the air-conditioning turned up high enough. You should go for a quick swim but don't stay in the sun too long."

Vanessa swallowed with difficulty. "What a good idea," she said, not looking at Kirk.

Thankfully another guest came into the reception area just then, and with Hugh still busy with the previous guest, Linda came around the counter. "Here, cuz. Let me take over. You go have that swim."

Vanessa didn't need further prompting. She twirled toward the door marked Private, desperate to grab any excuse to get out of that man's presence. She heard him tell the others he had to get home.

Then, "Vanessa?"

If only she could ignore him, but Linda and Hugh would think her rude.

She stopped and glanced over her shoulder. "Yes?"

"See you at the party," he said, an intensity to his eyes that made her softly gasp.

Somehow she managed a jerky nod before making her escape. It hadn't been an issue before now but tomorrow night she'd tell him he'd got it all wrong. He had to be told she was a widow. There was no way this man would want any involvement with a woman who was still mourning the man she loved.

Kirk Deverill would never accept being second best.

After six weeks away Kirk had looked forward to coming home but now as he drove toward Deverill Downs, he realized the news that his friends were leaving the area shouldn't really have come as a surprise. He'd miss them. There weren't many people he totally trusted like he did Hugh and Linda.

So why did his mind keep switching back to a beautiful, green-eyed woman with honey-blond hair? Tall and with a stunning figure, Vanessa Hamilton was a surprise find here in his hometown. A man would have to be six feet under not to want another look at those firm breasts, or at legs so long and slim they'd cling to him like warm sap on a gum tree.

He grimaced to himself. He was certainly waxing lyrical today. Being without a woman for a while did that to a man.

Okay, so that had been his choice, not the other way around. He'd gone to Sydney over a month ago to spend Christmas with his mother, who'd moved to the city after his father's death. Then his mother had needed an operation and he'd ended up staying longer than expected when there had been a complication. She was fine now, but he'd been glad to be there for her and his sister.

And all that had put a curb on his sex life. Strangely he hadn't cared. Running into a newly married Samantha, who'd made it clear she was quite willing to resume their affair, had left a bad taste in his mouth. He couldn't believe three months ago he'd been ready to ask her to marry him. She was the type of woman who hadn't wanted children and that had suited him perfectly. She'd lived in Sydney but he'd been certain she'd jump at the chance to marry him and move to the outback.

Instead she'd up and married one of his business acquaintances from the city, an older, richer guy who could give her more than "life" on a cattle station. The worse thing was that Kirk had known she would have married *him* if Marcus hadn't come along.

How could he have read Samantha so wrong? She'd put on such a classy act, duping him into believing they might come to love each other and have a decent life together. Thank God she'd dumped him before he'd told her he was sterile. At least she didn't have that power over him.

No woman ever would.

Bloody hell, he should have learned his lesson with Jillian and their one-night stand all those years ago at university. Claiming he was the father of her child when he'd known he'd used protection had made him suspicious and proven two things.

She was a liar.

And he was sterile.

Never would he fully trust another woman. Nor would he ever ask another woman to marry him, of that he was certain. He could have plenty of satisfying relationships without marriage. There were plenty of women who wanted nothing more than good company and good sex.

Even Vanessa Hamilton.

It wouldn't be merely good sex with her. It would be *great* sex. She was a feisty one, that one. All that fire flashing in those lovely green eyes, and the way her delicately shaped mouth had pursed with annoyance, she was just what he needed to warm his bed again. It made him wonder what else lay beneath that prickly skin of hers. No doubt about it, he was going to find out.

Two

Vanessa spent the rest of the day helping out around the motel. She, Linda and Hugh had perfected a routine of taking turns to look after Toby and Josh, taking them outside in the private garden area or playing on the living-room rug with the boys. If they were all busy, then one of the staff usually stepped in for a short time. She felt like she had the best of both worlds, and loved being able to help Linda and Hugh as well.

But tonight as she fed Josh his dinner, her heart was heavy, her mind awash with thoughts. Mike had been careless with money and no matter how hard she'd tried to save, he'd spent it as fast. They'd rented an apartment, their car had been on hire purchase, and they hadn't owned much. She'd eventually receive compensation money from Mike's death, but she planned on putting that into a trust account for Josh.

And none of that helped her situation right now. If she

returned to Sydney she'd have to find somewhere to live. And she'd have to get a job and put Josh in day care. Or she might have to let Grace and Rupert look after him. Or heaven help her, she and Josh might have to move in with them. Already they had him booked into the right school. It had the right type of people, they'd said, and he'd make the right type of friends.

Oh, God.

Suddenly she felt like she'd been cut adrift. It was the same feeling she'd had when her mother remarried five years ago and went to live in England. She hadn't met Mike then, and with her father having died when she was little, her job in an insurance office had been busy but it hadn't been enough. Linda had been living in Melbourne at the time, and Linda's four brothers and sisters were great cousins but they were older and had lives of their own. She'd felt so alone. Looking at alternatives now, she wasn't sure what was worse.

"You're quiet, sweetie," Linda said from where she sat on the sofa folding washing.

Vanessa winced inwardly as she looked across the open-plan living area to her dark-haired cousin. Was she so transparent?

"Just thinking," she said casually.

"You're not fretting too much about what you're going to do, are you? We'll think of something. I promise."

"You've got enough to worry about right now."

"So one more thing won't matter, will it?" she said, with more bravado than not, Vanessa thought. "In any case, we have a month before we have to leave here."

Vanessa nodded, then continued feeding her son. The best thing she could do for Linda right now was stay calm and pretend she was fine. She rather suspected Linda was doing the same thing for *her* sake.

"By the way," Linda said, after a few moments' pause, "what did you think of Kirk Deverill?"

Vanessa's mouth tightened. She hadn't known whether to say anything to her cousin but…

"You really shouldn't have asked him to keep me company tomorrow night. I'll be busy helping with the party." She didn't dare mention the dinner invitation. Wild horses wouldn't drag that out of her.

Linda's eyebrows rose in disbelief. "I don't believe it! The man's got a ton of money and he's a total hunk and you're *complaining* about spending time with him? Cuz, he's the catch of the century."

"And your point is?" Vanessa said with a touch of sarcasm, then immediately felt bad.

Linda stopped what she was doing, her eyes considering her from across the room. "You don't like him, do you?"

Vanessa went to speak her mind, then looked away to hand Josh the spoon to play with. She'd probably said enough. Kirk Deverill was too handsome for his own good and was quick to take advantage, but much as she wanted to, she wasn't so sure she should share her opinion with her cousin.

She shrugged. "I just don't know the guy, okay?"

Linda sighed. "Mike's been gone six months now, sweetie. You have to get on with your life."

Striving to ignore the empty void in her heart that the mention of her dead husband brought, Vanessa swallowed hard. Her cousin meant well. "I'm trying to get on with my life but that doesn't mean I want you to make dates for me."

"It wasn't meant as an actual date. I just thought it would do you good to see new people."

A bubble of warmth coiled around Vanessa's heart. Her cousin was a lovely person. "I know. And thanks. But I'm not ready. I'm not sure I'll ever be." Would she ever be able to ignore the fear in her heart? The fear of loving and losing.

"Of course, you could always stay home tomorrow night," Linda surprisingly suggested. "Phyllis's granddaughter said she'd babysit but you could look after Josh and Toby yourself. I could tell Kirk you're not feeling well or something."

It was tempting but somehow it smacked of cowardice and Kirk would see right through it. And besides, once he learned of her circumstances she was certain that would be the end of it.

"No, I'll be fine. I guess I can handle him for one night."

Linda winked at her as she stood up with the folded towels. "Sweetie, that man's worth more than a night."

Vanessa gave a weak smile and returned to feeding her son. She had the feeling her cousin was right.

The party was in full swing by the time Kirk arrived the next evening. He was late but he'd had no choice. His housekeeper, Martha, had decided she needed to go look after her sister. He'd made a booking then arranged for one of his men to drive her to Dubbo Airport, but she'd been upset so he'd stayed with her until it was time to leave. He'd never forget how she had helped his mother cope with his father's terminal illness.

And now he put all that out of his mind as he stood near the entrance and ordered a whiskey with one of the young males acting as a drink waiter for the night. The restaurant was crowded but there was only one person he wanted to see tonight.

Vanessa.

She was nowhere to be seen.

Just then, she came through the swinging kitchen door carrying a plate of hors d'oeuvres. An odd jolt shot through his chest. She looked incredible in a short black dress that fitted snugly against her breasts, its thin straps emphasizing her smooth neckline and shoulders, the color a glorious foil to the silken mass of her blond hair.

Without hesitation, he skirted the tables and caught up with her near a potted palm. Intense pleasure coursed through him when he saw the quick spurt of desire in those green eyes before she masked her expression.

She was even more beautiful tonight.

"Good evening, Mr. Deverill," she said with cool politeness.

He raised a mocking eyebrow. "Mister? I'm sure you called me by my name yesterday."

"I'm sure I called you a lot of things yesterday."

The comment made him laugh low and husky. Then, "You look fantastic tonight."

A blush ran over her cheeks.

Not so cool.

"Dance with me," he murmured, wanting nothing more than to hold her in his arms and feel her moving against him.

Her gaze darted out over the dance floor in the center of the room. "Dance?"

"Surely even Cinderella can have fun at the ball?" he teased.

"I—" She looked down at the plate and began rearranging the hors d'oeuvres, the faint tremor in her hand shooting satisfaction right through him.

Then she lifted her eyes and moistened her lips. "There's something I should—"

"Yes, there is," he said huskily.

Come closer and touch me. Slide your hands around my neck. Press yourself against me.

She drew in a quick breath. "I—" Raising her chin higher, she pulled back her shoulders, unknowingly emphasizing her firm, rounded breasts. "I've just got one thing to say to you, Mr. Deverill."

"What's that?"

"You are no prince." With that she took off into the throng.

Amused, Kirk watched the feminine sway of her hips. Then he exhaled a low rush of air. He'd have liked nothing better than to follow her. To slide that zipper open at the back of her dress. To plant kisses all along her spine. And beyond—

The waiter interrupted his thoughts with the glass of whiskey. He took a sip and it burned going down. A long, slow burn.

Just like Vanessa.

Then Hugh's parents called his name and the world intruded, but over the next hour he couldn't keep from watching Vanessa mix with the other guests. She smiled graciously. She laughed. And then she'd catch him looking at her and that smile would freeze on her lips, a signal that he affected her as much as she affected him.

Later she disappeared into the kitchen with a pile of dirty glasses. He followed and found her stacking the dishwasher. She was alone, as he'd hoped she would be. She couldn't know it, but she gave him a bird's-eye view of her cleavage, the same view he would get if she were lying on top of him. Two perfect globes. His to caress.

"Want some help?" he said huskily.

She straightened, a guarded look in her eyes. "Thanks, but I can manage." Spinning away, she picked up some clean plates from the table and reached for the top shelf of a cupboard.

He watched as her dress inched up her thighs. Damn, but she had gorgeous legs. Long and slim and firm enough for a man to grip as she rode him home, smooth enough for a man to slide up and into her.

"You owe me a dance, Vanessa."

Her eyelashes flickered, then her lips twisted. "I'm sure Phyllis would love to come back from her break and find us dancing in her kitchen," she scoffed, picking up more plates.

Unable to stand another look at those legs, he strode over and took the plates out of her hands, then put them on the shelf himself.

He turned and took slow steps toward her. "We could go outside under the stars, if you'd prefer."

Anywhere.

He didn't care.

As long as she was in his arms.

"No, I can't." She went to spin away.

He put his hand on her arm, stopping her. "One dance can't hurt us."

She tensed as if she knew one dance was all it would take. "Kirk, listen. This is all a waste of time."

"What is?" he murmured, watching the way she suddenly moistened her lips.

"You…trying to seduce me. It won't work. I can't do this."

He pulled her closer. "Vanessa, you're only fooling yourself if you think—"

"Kirk, I'm a widow."

He blinked in shock.

"My husband died six months ago."

He stared at her, trying to absorb the information.

"I've been trying to tell you. I—"

The screen door opened and Phyllis stepped inside the kitchen. "I don't believe it! Kirk Deverill in my kitchen," she scolded lightly, then stopped, her gaze going to Vanessa. "Oh, was I interrupting something?"

There was a pause but Kirk couldn't have spoken to save his life. A widow? She was too young. She was only in her mid-twenties.

Vanessa stepped back. "Not at all, Phyllis," she assured the motel cook, then headed for a side door. "I'll leave you two to catch up." She left the room.

Kirk let her go. He had to. He couldn't make his feet move right then.

"So how's your mother, Kirk? I want to hear all about her."

Hell, what could he say to Vanessa anyway?

"And Martha?" Phyllis added. "I believe her sister isn't well."

Kirk slowly turned back to the older woman, forcibly pulling himself together, but his mind was working overtime. He still couldn't believe Vanessa was a widow.

Christ!

Vanessa was shaking by the time she left the kitchen and slipped into Linda's bathroom. She'd told him. He knew now. He wouldn't pursue her further. And that was just as well. Tonight had the signs of being a prelude to a relationship she wasn't ready for.

A man-woman relationship.

All she had to do was get through the rest of the evening.

Drawing a calming breath, she left the safety of the bathroom and took a few minutes to chat to the teenager babysitting the boys here in Linda's private quarters. Then she took a quick peek in on a sleeping Josh before heading back to the party.

On entering the restaurant, the first thing she saw was Kirk dancing with a young, raven-haired beauty whose father owned a sheep station not far from town. She gazed up at Kirk as if any minute she'd swoon at his feet.

A touch of cynicism seeped inside Vanessa. He didn't seem to be worried about *his* attraction for *her* right now, with Tina's red dress clinging to his dark trousers. Any closer and they'd be joined at the hip.

"Like to dance, Vanessa?" a male voice said beside her, and she looked up to see Seth Collins, one of the other woman's brothers, standing there, his brown eyes reflecting admiring lights.

She flashed him a smile, glad to have someone take her mind off Kirk. "Lead the way." On the dance floor she went into his arms. His height forced her to look up at him and he grinned down at her with a face as handsome as his sister's was beautiful.

Vanessa smiled right back at him, aware that he found her desirable. Unfortunately he did nothing for her. Not like...

Her gaze shot past him to Kirk, who was scowling at her over Tina's shoulder. There was a determined look in his eyes and suddenly she wasn't sure being emotionally tied up in her late husband would make any difference to him. Kirk Deverill went after whatever or whoever he wanted.

She dragged her eyes away. "Had enough to eat, Seth?"

He nodded. "Best spread I've had in a long time."

She darted a quick look back at Kirk, who was still looking at her.

And he was getting closer.

Her heart thudded in her chest. She should have known he was the type of man who let nothing get in his way.

Swallowing, she quickly looked at Seth again. "Had enough to drink?"

"More than enough, thanks."

Kirk was closing in on them, a hard set to his jaw. Nervously she scraped an imaginary strand of hair off her cheek. "Good. We aim to please."

Seth gave a short laugh that grated on her taut nerves. "You do a good job of looking after your guests."

Closer still.

"Er...that's because everyone's been so nice to me."

"I'm sure you're easy to be ni—"

"Seth," Kirk interrupted, coming right up beside them, "you'd better take your sister outside. She says she's going to be sick."

Tina hiccupped.

"Great," Seth said ruefully but he immediately released Vanessa and put his arms around Tina. "Come on, sis. Let's get you some fresh air." He shrugged at Vanessa regretfully. "Sorry about this."

"That's okay." Vanessa began edging as far away from Kirk as possible. "I have to go check on—"

Kirk pulled her into his arms, wrapping her in his warmth. "We need to talk," he rasped, and began leading her around the floor as Seth escorted his sister to the door.

Vanessa pulled herself together. "Do you often make women sick when they dance with you?" she said sweetly, not wanting him to know he had her running scared.

His eyes dismissed her comment. "Tell me about your husband," he all but growled.

Like a flash she grasped that this wasn't about him pursuing her. All he wanted were answers, nothing more. She could understand that. Most people were curious when they discovered someone so young had been widowed.

Tension eased out of her shoulders. "Mike was a policeman. He was killed in a bank robbery six months ago." She could count it down to the weeks, days, hours. She would remember the exact date and time for the rest of her life.

A muscle jerked in his jaw. "Hell, I'm sorry."

"Thank you." She'd heard those words so many times from people, and she appreciated them. Yet hearing them come from this man made her feel strange.

"How long were you married?"

Vanessa swallowed. "Two years."

His hand tightened on her hip. "And were you happy?"

"Very," was all she could manage, otherwise she'd be thinking about Mike and how much she missed him. And it didn't seem right to be thinking about him while she was dancing in the arms of another man.

His mouth compressed. "Why didn't you tell me sooner?"

She didn't like his tone. "I don't believe I owe you any details of my private life," she snapped.

Another couple danced too close and he had to move her out of the way. By the time she fell back into step, she hoped he'd let the subject of her marriage go.

He didn't.

His eyes snagged hers, almost accusingly. "Why aren't you wearing any rings?"

She'd *known* he'd noticed. "I've taken them off temporarily. They were too tight in the heat."

Those blue eyes gave her the laser treatment. "You knew I thought you were available."

Her lips twisted. "You probably think *every* woman is available."

"Aren't they?" he mocked.

She sucked in a sharp breath at his arrogance. The road to Sydney must be littered with women who threw themselves at him, but that was no excuse for—

Just then, she saw Cindy standing near the kitchen door carrying her son. "Josh!" She immediately forgot Kirk as she left his arms and hurried over to the babysitter. "Is something wrong? What's the matter?" She didn't know what she'd do if anything happened to him.

"I think he heard your voice before. He started crying and won't settle." Cindy pulled a face. "I'm sorry to drag you away."

"Don't be," Vanessa said, lifting Josh in her arms, relieved he wasn't sick. His eyes were wet from crying. She kissed his cheek and smoothed the blond hair off his forehead. "How's Toby?"

"Sound asleep," Cindy said. "I'd better get back to him. Do you want me to take Josh back? He might settle now that he's seen you."

"No, that's fine. I think I'll take him home now." It was getting late and she needed no better excuse to get out of here.

Cindy nodded, then disappeared through the kitchen door.

Vanessa hugged Josh closer, smelling his soft, sweet scent. "Time to take you home and put you to bed, little man." She turned around to find Linda or Hugh and tell them that she was leaving so they wouldn't worry.

She froze. *Kirk.* He'd followed her.

His eyes had an odd glitter. "He's yours?"

She swallowed then nodded, proud of her son but feeling the awkwardness of the moment.

"I'll carry him for you," he said in a brusque voice.

She stiffened. "No, the apartment's only out the back."

"You could fall over in those heels," he said, making her aware he missed nothing about her.

Suddenly she had to get out of here…away from the restaurant…away from Kirk Deverill. She had to keep a physical distance, if only to maintain an emotional one.

"No, I'll be fine."

He said something low under his breath. "I insist." His eyes held hers. He wasn't going to give up.

She expelled a shaky sigh. "Okay, but I have to find Linda first and tell her I've gone."

"She's over near the bar."

She looked and saw Linda near the bar, standing beneath the Happy Anniversary banner. Her cousin waved at them and Vanessa indicated she was taking Josh home, and received a speculative look and a nod of acknowledgment.

Then she let Kirk lift Josh from her arms, half expecting Josh to cry—and wishing he would—only he didn't. Then she and Kirk left via the kitchen. Phyllis and a waitress looked up as they passed through, but Vanessa gave a bright smile and hoped she wasn't tomorrow's gossip. And if she was then it was only one person's fault.

His.

Looking directly ahead, she didn't talk as her high heels tapped along the well-lit driveway until they came to the converted garage. Once inside the apartment, she waited until Kirk placed Josh in his crib, then she tucked her son in and moved back into the living room. She saw Kirk's gaze as he took in the room with its polished wood floor, comfortable sofa and handmade cushions.

For a long moment his blue eyes rested on the wedding photograph of her and Mike, who'd been so handsome in his policeman's uniform.

She swallowed the lump in her throat. "Thanks for carrying Josh for me."

He drew his gaze away from the photograph and looked at her, an unreadable expression in his eyes. "No problem."

Trying to look experienced at this sort of thing, she walked toward him and held out her hand. "I guess this is good night."

His hand slid over hers like a glove. "I guess it is."

She realized her mistake then. She hadn't wanted to touch him. Hadn't wanted to feel his skin against her own, not even in the most casual way.

And she knew that wasn't true.

She *wanted* to touch him.

And there would be nothing cavalier about it.

Something must have shown on her face because he gave a sharp intake of breath. The next instant he brought her hand to his mouth and ever so slowly he kissed the inside of her wrist.

Heat arrowed into her belly, igniting her blood like she had never known before, not even with Mike. Loving Mike had been simple and uncomplicated. Somehow she knew it wouldn't be like that with Kirk.

He dropped her hand and stepped back. "Goodbye, Vanessa," he said thickly, and moved toward the front door.

Then he was gone.

The door shut behind him.

She stood there shaking. Then, stunned by what just one touch could do to her, she collapsed on the couch, her thoughts tumbling down like the house made of straw. Now that she was alone, she wanted him back, wanted him to touch her more, make love to her.

Oh, Lord. What was the matter with her? Mike was still her husband in her heart; meanwhile she longed to hop into bed with the first good-looking man that had come along. What had happened to remaining true to Mike's memory? The father of her child. Kirk Deverill dredged up emotions she intended to keep hidden. Emotions of desire and need that shouldn't be there. Her husband had only been dead six months. How could she yearn to be held close by someone else so soon? A stranger no less.

Her heart squeezed with pain but she didn't cry. The season had come and gone for more tears.

And this feeling for Kirk?

It, too, would pass.

An hour later Vanessa still hadn't fallen asleep. She felt wound up, like a mouse running around one of those exercise wheels. Perhaps a few slow laps of the pool would relax her.

Pushing herself out of bed, she peeked out her bedroom

window. The glow of night-lights showed the pool area empty of people, with most of the motel guests having retired for the night and others still at the party on the other side of the motel. With the pool close enough to keep an eye on her apartment, she didn't need any further encouragement to slip into her one-piece swimsuit.

Five minutes later, pleased that out here the party sounded as though it had wound down some and that Kirk would probably have left, she dropped her towel on a deck chair and carefully descended the steps at the corner of the pool.

As she eased in up to her neck, ripples fanned out around her and the reflections of the dimmed lights gently bounced over the surface of the water. For a few seconds she enjoyed the anointment, the warm lotion of the water massaging her body, helping her to unwind.

Then she kicked off from the wall of the pool and started to swim, keeping as quiet as possible as she sliced smoothly through the water, not wanting anyone to join her and spoil this for her.

Twenty laps later she felt tired but at last she felt refreshed. Rolling onto her back in the middle of the pool, she looked up at the night sky. The darkened shape of a bird flew across the silhouette of the moon. Stars twinkled down on her from a bed of velvet. An owl hooted in the distance. This was the life. She could so get used to—

"You came to Jackaroo Plains for a reason, didn't you?" a deep male voice said.

She swallowed water and began to choke. Her peace shattered, she tried to catch her breath as her feet touched the bottom of the pool to stand up. In a dimly lit area in the corner, Kirk sat on one of the deck chairs. Had he been there all along?

"Are you following me?" she demanded.

"No. I was out here already."

Her breath suspended in midair. The thought of him watching her slowly step into the pool surrounded by night-lights, seeing her body outlined by the one-piece she wore, made her quiver inside.

"And you didn't answer my question," he reminded her.

"What question was that?"

"You came here to help get over your grief, didn't you? That's why Linda's so concerned about you."

No need to tell him about her in-laws. It was none of his business. "Linda worries too much."

He got to his feet and strolled toward the pool. "So what will you do when they sell the motel? Go back to Sydney?"

She didn't know what she was going to do. "I'm working on something now," she fibbed, not wanting him to know how desperate she felt. She turned the conversation away from her. "Anyway, why are you out here? I thought you'd be enjoying the party."

He stood looking down at her, watching the moonlit water lap at the top of her breasts, his strong features holding a certain sensuality that made her shiver. "I needed some fresh air."

Pretending his husky voice didn't perturb her, she eased backward in the water, slowly moving around, trying to look unaffected by him.

"I guess you'll be heading home soon then," she said, hoping against hope that he'd take the hint.

"I've booked a room for the night."

She stopped moving. Had he expected to share it with someone? Her? This was his friends' motel, but he would be discreet, she knew.

All at once she became conscious of feeling a tiny bit cold but she didn't want to get out of the pool in front of him. He'd seen more than enough of her tonight.

He frowned. "You're getting cold. Come on, I'll help you

out of there." All action now, he went and picked up her towel from the chair.

Her heartbeat started to skip. "No, it's okay. I'm fine. I'll just swim around some more then go back to my apartment. No need for you to wait around."

His frown deepened. "I'm not leaving you here alone, Vanessa. You could get a cramp."

"I won't." She hoped she didn't sound as desperate as she felt, but suspected she did. "You really should be going back to the party."

A very masculine look suddenly entered his eyes. "I should?" He paused. "Why?"

She drew an unsteady breath. "Er…why?" Her throat closed up. Her mind froze. She couldn't think of a thing to say that didn't give away how much he was affecting her.

Then a mask came down over his face. "Come on, Vanessa. Get out of the pool." Clearly remote now, he opened the towel and held it up for her.

She wavered.

"Vanessa?"

She stared at him, then told herself he was only concerned for her welfare, nothing else. It was either that or she'd never get out of the pool.

She dared not look at him as she concentrated on moving through the water toward him. Her foot found the first step and she began to rise out of the pool. She could feel his eyes on her as the water sluiced down over her swimsuit, each step up exposing every inch of her body to him.

She reached the top step and looked up.

Their eyes locked.

The air stilled between them.

He moved closer. "Let me," he murmured, standing in front of her, slipping it around her shoulders.

Her heart slammed against her ribs. "Um...you might get wet."

"I don't mind." He pulled the edges of the towel tight at the column of her throat, bringing her closer, against him.

Their bodies touched.

Sizzled.

She felt him all the way down to her toes.

Suddenly she saw tiny flames in his eyes and an ache that had been growing all night throbbed through her veins. She wanted to touch the full curve of his mouth with her own just once, to taste its warmth, its strength.

He lowered his head and she trembled, and with a silent sigh, closed her eyes as his mouth covered hers. Her lips met his and he kissed her...and kissed her more...long and slow. Oddly enough her lips felt as if they were welcoming him home. He tasted both familiar yet unsettling, firm yet gentle. A heady mixture of the known and unknown.

He drew her closer, cupping the back of her head and deepening the kiss. Then groaning a low sound that seemed to wrench from deep inside him, he pulled her hips tightly against his arousal, letting her know what he wanted. She leaned into him, reveling in the sexual heat which spread like bushfire from his body to hers. She decided then and there that he felt as good as he looked. And she moved closer still. Need was everything. She needed more than the taste of his mouth. More than the feel of her breasts against his hard chest. She needed to feel him inside her. For the first time ever she understood why they called it consummation.

She wanted to be *consumed* by him.

Without warning, he broke away, breathing heavily, his eyes smoldering for her. A pulse leaped along the hard line of his jaw. "Vanessa, go," he rasped.

She swallowed over the lump in her throat. "I—"

"Go."

She didn't need to be told a second time. Whirling around, she ran back to her apartment as fast as her legs would take her. When she finally closed the door behind her, she sank to her knees and brought her hand to her mouth. Dear God, what had she done? Everything she'd believed about herself and the type of woman she was had just been proven wrong.

She had betrayed Mike.

Worse. She'd kissed another man and found something in that kiss she'd never found in the two years of loving her husband.

Lust.

She had wanted to melt in Kirk's arms and have him carry her off to bed and a night of whirlwind passion and blessed satiation. Except that Kirk hadn't given her the chance, had he? No thanks to her, she thought with self-deprecation.

So shouldn't that make her happy?

Yes.

Why, then, did she have an inexplicable feeling of emptiness? As if she'd lost something important she'd never really had.

Kirk had a raw feeling in his gut as he let himself into his motel room. The party was over for him in more ways than one. The woman he was so attracted to…the woman he'd wanted to make his own…was not only a grieving widow but a mother as well.

Why the friggin' hell hadn't someone thought to mention it yesterday? He wouldn't have come here tonight. He wouldn't have gotten involved. Now he had the taste of Vanessa Hamilton in his mouth.

And the imprint of her body on his clothes.

Dammit, the last thing he wanted to see right now was his reflection in the mirror. He was wet all the way from his

blazer and shirt down to the front of his trousers, the damp-
ness touching his skin through the material. His pulse quickened. Just looking at himself reminded him what she'd felt
like in his arms. Soft and willowy, her curves flush against
him.

Not that he'd forget in any hurry.

Just like he wouldn't forget she was a young widow with
a small child. No question now why she'd been fighting his
advances. She was still getting over the death of her husband.
And he intended to leave her to it.

Of course all that begged the question.

If she hadn't felt anything for *him*, what exactly had she
been fighting?

Three

Vanessa had a very restless night, so the next morning the last thing she wanted to hear when she picked up the office telephone was her mother-in-law's voice on the other end of the line. Guilt immediately washed over her. She'd been married to this woman's son—and she'd kissed another man last night.

"How is my little Joshua doing?"

Vanessa shuddered. The thrice-weekly phone calls were getting too much. And he wasn't *her* Joshua at all.

"He's fine, Grace," she said, keeping her tone neutral.

"We miss him."

"I know you do." They could at least agree on that.

"Did you receive the parcel of special baby cereal I sent for him? I know you like feeding him that cheap brand but I'm told this one is the most nutritional for a child his age."

Vanessa held back a wince. The baby cereal she fed Josh

was a good brand off the supermarket shelf. And it wasn't too cheap either. "Yes, it arrived. Thank you."

"And did the clothes fit him? I bought them from one of the best stores in the city. I don't want him looking like nobody cares about him."

Vanessa swallowed back a retort at the dig. "The clothes fit just fine, Grace." They were expensive and nice for going out, but not for everyday use.

"Good."

All at once Vanessa was aware of Linda in the reception area. They knew each other so well and it was hard keeping anything from her cousin. Linda had already mentioned how she'd seen Kirk leave the party with her last night, and how he hadn't come back, but there had been no insinuation in the comment, despite her curiosity. Linda knew she didn't bed-hop.

"We have some exciting news," Grace's voice cut across her thoughts. "Nadine is pregnant."

"Really?" She was genuinely happy for her sister-in-law. "That's wonderful. You must be pleased."

"We are." Then Grace gave a shaky sigh. "If only Michael was here. He'd be over the moon for his sister."

Vanessa took a breath. "Yes." Mike had loved his sister.

How close was Kirk to his own sister? she wondered, then forced herself to dismiss her thoughts. What Kirk Deverill and his family were to each other didn't matter to her. She just hoped he checked out of his room and went home soon. It put her on edge knowing he was here in the motel somewhere.

"Grace, I must go now." She listened further. "Yes, I'll give Josh a big hug from you and Rupert." She hung up and took a deep breath to steady herself. Her in-laws always made her uneasy.

Linda came to the doorway. "She never asks how you're doing, does she? It's always about Josh."

Vanessa shrugged. "She knows I'm okay."

"You're too generous."

Vanessa rather thought Grace would say she wasn't generous enough, especially where Josh was concerned. The older couple would take him from her in a heartbeat.

"Generous or not, I'd better get back to cleaning those motel rooms. It was a full house last night and—"

"I've got it!" Linda said, springing forward into the office. "Oh, why didn't I think of this before?" She broke into a big smile. "You're coming with us to Queensland, sweetie."

Vanessa came around the desk. "What?"

"I can't let you and Josh go back to your in-laws. We'll find you an apartment close to us and I'll look after Josh if you need to get a job."

Vanessa's heart thudded for a moment before reality set in. "Thanks for thinking of me, Linda, but it wouldn't be fair on either you or Hugh. Or Toby. You're starting a new life. You'll have responsibilities that go with Hugh's new job as caretaker. You don't need me adding to the mix."

Linda made a dismissive gesture. "You wouldn't be adding to anything."

"And what if you're pregnant? You told me you had terrible morning sickness with Toby. Can you imagine looking after *two* infants as well as feeling nauseated and off-color?" Vanessa shook her head. "No, it's a lovely offer but I can't accept."

Her cousin's face began to fall. "Well, perhaps you could put Josh in day care. I know it's not ideal but—"

"I don't think I can afford an apartment as well as day care," Vanessa said gently, hating to shoot her cousin down.

Just then there was a noise at the doorway and they both looked around to see Kirk and Hugh entering the office.

"You two look serious," Hugh said, a question in his eyes,

but it was the flat look in Kirk's eyes that made Vanessa's gaze dart away. Their kiss last night should not have happened.

"We've been discussing Vanessa's situation."

Vanessa could feel her cheeks warm. The last thing she wanted was to discuss this in front of Kirk. "Linda, please, I'll sort things out."

Her cousin sighed. "I wish you could at least stay here."

"I doubt the new owner would want me living in his motel without paying the full rate."

"We could ask him to give you a job."

"I can't see that happening. You said yourself he'd be making cutbacks."

Linda's shoulders sagged. "But I can't stand the thought of you going back to those awful in-laws of yours."

Vanessa shifted a look at Kirk and saw his eyes sharpen. She groaned inwardly. "They're not that bad," she managed to joke.

"Aren't they?"

Vanessa forced a smile at both Linda and Hugh. "Something will turn up. I'm sure of it."

And if it didn't, then perhaps it was best that she did return to Sydney. And soon for Linda's sake. And she would find a way to stop her parents-in-law from smothering Josh.

She would.

"Honestly, there's no need to worry about me. We still have a month to sort things out." Then a thought occurred to her and she grabbed at it for the moment. "I might even be able to find a job somewhere in the area. It doesn't have to be at the motel. I'm pretty good at waiting on tables and I'm not bad at cooking and cleaning, either." She smiled at her cousin with more confidence than she felt.

Linda's brows pulled together. "But where would you live?"

"I'll advertise. Someone might even have a spare room where I can board. It doesn't have to be in Jackaroo Plains."

She really liked the town but it wouldn't be a good idea with Kirk close by. "There's plenty of other places on the map, you know."

"Hey, that's a good idea, Vanessa," Hugh agreed.

Vanessa smiled. "Thanks."

"I guess that's a possibility," Linda was saying, as if to herself.

"Sure it is," Vanessa added, trying to be enthusiastic. "I'm sure lots of people would welcome not only the company but the extra income as well." She realized Kirk was watching them with a frown and she smiled at him, hoping he'd help put Linda's mind at rest. "Isn't that right, Kirk? There would be plenty of people looking for someone to share with, don't you think?"

He seemed to stiffen before speaking. "Yes, I suppose there would be."

Linda looked at her cousin with restrained enthusiasm. "We'd have to find someone good and decent. I don't want you staying with just anyone."

Vanessa could relax for a while now. "I wouldn't, I promise. I'd make sure I checked it out thoroughly before accepting any offer."

"Good idea. And Hugh and Kirk have a lot of connections. They might know of someone who can take you in." She looked at the men. "Isn't that right, guys?" She turned back to Vanessa. "We'll make sure you and Josh…" Unexpectedly her words trailed away and an odd light entered her eyes.

Vanessa suspected some problem had occurred to Linda, but for now she'd had enough. "Great." She leaned up and kissed her cousin's cheek, touched by her concern. "Now I'd better go finish those rooms so they'll be ready for tonight."

Giving them all a sweeping smile, she headed for the door, making her escape without incident but surprised by the hard look in Kirk's eyes as she passed him.

It was almost as if she'd done something wrong.

* * *

Kirk watched Vanessa walk away. He should have known what she was planning the minute he stepped inside the room. She didn't want to return to Sydney and she needed somewhere to live, so she had no compunction in using him. He'd watched her work Linda like an expert, with all that talk about being good at cooking and cleaning and how she'd be looking to share a house with someone *in the area*.

Him.

It was clear she was angling for his housekeeper job and had no problem using her cousin to get it.

Women! Were they all the same? Jillian. Samantha. Now Vanessa. He'd expected more from her for some reason. He'd thought she'd have the integrity not to use a man for her own purposes, whether those purposes were for a valid reason or not. How could he have read her so wrong?

"Oh, my God, I've just realized something."

Kirk stiffened. *Here it comes,* he thought. Linda had fallen for it hook, line and sinker, piecing it together as if it was all her idea. Exactly as Vanessa had known she would.

Linda's eyes were lit with excitement. "Oh, God, Kirk, Vanessa would be perfect to replace Martha, don't you think? Heavens, I can't believe I'm only thinking of it now. Phyllis told me last night at the party that Martha left yesterday to stay with her sister for six months. I should have thought of it then."

His jaw clenched. "Sorry, but that's not a good idea."

Linda blinked at him. "Wh-what?"

He hated to disappoint her but he didn't want Vanessa living in his house. She was too much temptation. And too much trouble. Nothing good would come of them being stuck together in an isolated house for six months. Not now he knew she was a widow.

"I'm sorry, Linda," he said, encompassing Hugh in his words. "I know she's your cousin but I don't think it would work out."

A frown marred Linda's forehead. "I don't understand. Why not? She's a wonderful person and a good worker. I can vouch for her. So can Hugh. Can't you, Hugh?" She paused but not enough to give her husband time to respond. "If it's because of Josh, he's not a problem. He's a good little boy."

Kirk ignored a jolt. He'd never told his friends about his condition. It was just something so private...so personal. "I'm sure he is."

"You don't understand how important this is. I'm worried about her. I don't think she's ready to go back to Sydney. She's been here less than a month and that's not enough time for Josh's grandparents to cut the apron strings. Grace is still phoning here every couple of days. And it's always about Josh, never Vanessa."

Kirk didn't like the sound of that, but perhaps Linda was overreacting. Surely Vanessa's in-laws couldn't be *that* bad?

And if they were, it still wasn't up to him to sort out Vanessa's family problems. If Vanessa came to live with him—correction, to live in his house—she'd have more problems than her in-laws. Despite the attraction between them, she wasn't ready for a physical relationship.

And that was *all* he wanted.

Hugh put his hand on his wife's shoulder. "Darling, Kirk might already have someone else in mind."

She shook her head. "You don't, Kirk, do you? You told Phyllis you would have to look for someone." All at once her eyes riveted on him. "I know there's something going on between the two of you. It's as plain as the freckles on my nose. But you've got to look beyond that. You're her only hope. Don't turn your back on her now."

Silence rent the air, then Hugh growled, "Linda, shut up."

Kirk heard him but knew nothing would shut Linda up when she was protecting one of her own. "That's a low blow, Linda." She must know not too many people would get away with saying something like that to him.

She held his gaze. "I know, but this is too important to me. And to Vanessa and Josh."

He lifted a brow. "Are you sure you're not trying to ease your own guilt?"

She sucked in a sharp breath. "You certainly know how to give as good as you get." Then she recovered quickly with a challenge in her eyes that reminded him of Vanessa. "So, what's the verdict?"

Kirk looked at his friends. He loved Linda like a sister but even sisters were women who liked to manipulate men. And he knew Hugh would support his wife in this, even if he didn't agree with her.

All this for one woman.

Vanessa looked up from making the bed and caught her breath. Kirk stood leaning against the doorjamb of the vacant motel room.

"Well done, Vanessa," he said with a cynical twist to his lips and a hard look in his eyes that shocked her.

She frowned as she straightened. "What do you mean?"

"You must know I need a housekeeper."

She nodded. "I know your housekeeper's sister is sick."

"And yesterday Martha took six months off and flew to Adelaide to look after her." He gave an eloquent pause. "As I told Phyllis last night."

She was puzzled. "I don't understand. What's that got to do with me?"

"Everything."

She blinked. "I don't get what you're saying."

He pushed away from the door and came a few steps into the room. "Last night I asked you what you were going to do about your situation and you said you were working on something. That was after you heard the news about Martha, no doubt." He gave a harsh laugh. "Of course, I didn't know you meant you were working on *me*."

She felt her eyes go wide. "Wh-what? I wasn't."

"And just now with Linda, you were perfect. All that talk about cooking and cleaning and about someone with a spare room where you can board, then asking me what I thought."

"But I didn't mean anything by that. I was just trying to—"

"I know what you were trying to do. And it worked, as you knew it would. Linda thinks it's the perfect solution for you to be my housekeeper for six months."

"What!" This was ridiculous. How could Linda think such a thing? Or him?

There was something else they needed to take into account, too. "What about my son?"

"He won't be a problem," he said, his expression closed.

She swallowed hard. He had to know that being his housekeeper was the last thing she would want. Working for him would bring him too close. She wouldn't—couldn't—live under the same roof as him.

"Just forget what Linda said then."

"I can't forget it. She and Hugh mean a lot to me. I won't lose their friendship because of you."

She winced inwardly. Why was she suddenly the scum of the earth? "They wouldn't hold it against you."

"Really? Linda loves you like a sister. If you go anywhere else and things don't work out, then it's going to wreck our friendship. You know it and so do I." His features set with absolute determination. "I won't allow that to happen."

The breath caught in her throat. She understood him

wanting to protect his friendship with Linda and Hugh, but this wasn't *her* fault. How could things get so muddled so quickly?

"I need you to start as soon as possible," he said in clipped tones, dragging her back to the moment. "I'll give you a couple of days to wrap up things here. I'm sure Linda will understand," he added, his lip curling.

She hated his derision. And his unfounded accusations. She had done nothing wrong and that made angry bile rise in her throat.

She lifted her chin. "No, thanks. You can keep your job. I don't accept charity. And I certainly don't accept anything that's begrudgingly given."

A hint of something that could be admiration flickered in his eyes before vanishing. "So *you're* going to tell Linda that you refused my offer then."

She swallowed hard as she remembered her cousin's anxiety. "That's not fair."

He shrugged. "I'm only telling you that *I'm* not going to be held responsible for upsetting Linda further or for her thinking I didn't ask you." His eyes didn't leave her face. "You can go back to Sydney or not, but the job offer is there."

But he wished it wasn't *her* who needed the job, she silently inserted.

"By the way, it's not charity," he added. "I do need a housekeeper for six months. You'll have plenty of privacy. Your rooms would be on the other side of the house with your own bathroom."

Her shoulders slumped. It would have been best if Kirk *did* have a problem with her son. Then they'd both have an excuse not to even consider her going to live at his cattle station.

And then what?

Panic stirred in Vanessa's chest for her son. Did she really want to drag Josh back to the city after only a few weeks away? Or to another country town? And did she want to give up all the one-on-one time she had with Josh right now? She would have to juggle every moment between work and home, time that would be better spent with Josh, at least for six more months. His childhood was too precious.

For her son she would change her mind.

"Okay then, I accept."

Something dark pooled in his eyes before he said dryly, "Use a bit more enthusiasm when you tell Linda, will you?"

She ignored that. "There's one condition though."

His eyes narrowed. "What's that?"

Had he forgotten their kiss? Had he forgotten how much they'd wanted each other last night? She hadn't.

"You're not to touch me." It was a knee-jerk response, but she felt vulnerable where he was concerned. She needed a guarantee to help her keep her emotions safeguarded. "I'll be there to work, Kirk. Nothing more, nothing less."

He watched her in silence for a few seconds. "I have no intention of touching you again. It'll be a working relationship and that's all."

"Good. We understand each other now."

He turned away but all at once he turned back. A pulse beat in his cheek. "By the way. I promise not to touch you again, Vanessa. I haven't promised not to want you."

Two days later, Vanessa sat beside Kirk as he drove his Range Rover toward Deverill Downs. Waves of thirsty grass kept them company on either side of the road; inside the vehicle low music played in the background while Josh slept in the new infant seat Kirk had installed. Apart from asking her if she was comfortable or needed anything, he didn't speak.

The angry vibes were still bouncing off him, though they weren't as frequent, but they were still there below the surface.

It didn't bode well for the next six months, and Vanessa now regretted not having this out with Linda. In hindsight she should have said something during the past two days, but Linda had been so relieved about it all that she hadn't had the heart. Besides, Linda probably wouldn't have listened anyway. Her cousin was the headstrong one of the family, Vanessa mused with affection.

"Something funny?"

Vanessa blinked, then shook her head. "No, nothing," she said, aware that he probably thought she was congratulating herself on fooling him.

Sheesh!

An hour later, and having seen only one car, they turned onto a winding dirt road that appeared to lead nowhere. A few miles farther in, tall gum trees began to pepper the side of the road, creating an avenue of trees that took them right up to the homestead.

She gasped softly when she saw the house and its setting. Long and sprawling with a deep verandah appearing to go all the way around, it was enclosed by a well-kept garden and a front lawn that could only be green from underground water brought up by an artesian bore. In a landscape baked brown by the sun, it truly looked like an oasis in the desert. Definitely a Blue Ribbon property.

"This is lovely," she murmured, as he pulled up on the driveway. "Very…" She thought for a word. "Gentrified."

He shot her a cynical look. "Glad you like it."

For the sake of peace she bit back an angry comment as she hopped out of the vehicle and he did the same. Just then his cell phone rang and he answered it, while she went to the backseat and unbuckled Josh.

He finished his call. "I have to go. There's a small emergency over at the cattle yards with the calves," he said, all business now. He indicated a direction. "The manager's residence and workmen cottages are about a mile away over there, and the cattle yards are behind them." He opened the rear door of the Range Rover as he spoke. "Do you think you can look after yourself?"

"Of course. Josh and I will be fine." It would be a relief to be out of his presence.

"I'll put your luggage up here for now." He lifted out two suitcases and placed them on the verandah, then went and got the playpen she'd brought with her. Josh wasn't walking yet but he could crawl very fast and the playpen would keep him out of mischief. Everything else Kirk had said would be supplied for a small child, and she figured they were probably on loan from one of his employees and their family. "Take a look around. Your bedrooms are at the back of the house on the right and you'll find plenty to eat. I'm not sure what time I'll get back." He carried the last two suitcases. "Martha left a list of instructions and one of the wives has left a casserole in the fridge for tonight's dinner."

At least she didn't have to rush to find her feet.

He transferred a few more items, then he got back into the Range Rover. "If you need me, call me on my cell phone. Martha wrote the number down with the instructions."

And Martha was obviously Wonder Woman, Vanessa mused, as she stood there with Josh in her arms and watched Kirk drive off. She sighed. At least she could be pleased about one thing. Kirk's comments were that of an employer to employee.

Which they were, of course.

And that was exactly how it would stay, she told herself as she went inside to take a look around her new *temporary* home.

The house was generous in proportion. On one side there were formal living and dining rooms and a wood-paneled study. There were six bedrooms with ensuites, one of which was a very feminine room that must be his sister's. And there were two very masculine bedrooms, one lived in—Kirk's—and one that looked as if it hadn't been used for years.

Curious.

In a wing farther along, there was the main bedroom with a sitting area. She assumed it had been his parents' bedroom, especially when she saw a framed photograph of two teenage boys and a young girl. One of the boys was obviously Kirk and the other looked like him so she assumed he had a brother, which would explain the other masculine bedroom. The girl must be their sister, Jade.

The kitchen was on the other side of the house and was a total delight. It had magnificent granite bench tops and Italian floor tiles and all the latest appliances. A child's high chair that looked brand-new sat in one corner, surprising her. She'd thought for sure the furniture would be secondhand. Kirk must have really pulled out all the stops to get them bought and sent here in time.

There was also a decent-size bedroom that had a small sitting area with a television and DVD player, which she assumed had been for the housekeeper. In the smaller bedroom next to it, there was a crib for Josh that looked new as well. She was touched by Kirk's thoughtfulness. He was certainly determined to accommodate her son's needs in a nice way.

At the center rear of the house was a family sunroom, with an informal dining room close to the kitchen, but it was the dining table that brought an empty ache to her heart. Having been an only child, she'd always loved the idea of a big family sitting around the table, sharing their lives. Linda had been lucky in that respect. She'd had brothers and sisters. But with *her* father dead and it having been only Vanessa and her mother, it had never happened.

It was just a dream now, of course. Mike was gone, and Grace and Rupert didn't exactly fit the image of the extended family she had in her mind. They didn't want to *share* her life. They wanted to *control* it.

Just thinking about her parents-in-law made her uneasy as she carried her things inside and unpacked. She'd telephoned them this morning determined to tell them about her new job, but in the end she hadn't been able to bring herself to mention it. She would have to do it eventually, but right now she didn't need the recriminations or emotional blackmail Grace would inflict on her.

She sighed. At best, if she called them three times a week, she'd probably have some vital time to herself before needing to come clean. Only if they called the motel and someone other than Linda or Hugh answered the phone would they learn the truth. Her cousin and Hugh certainly wouldn't tell them.

Kirk didn't arrive back until seven. She heard the Range Rover drive around the side of the house, and he came into the kitchen looking ruggedly handsome, his face bronzed by the sun's rays. He was enough to make any woman catch her breath.

For a moment he just stood there looking at her, his eyes dark and hooded, until she could feel a blush start in her neck. Thankfully his gaze moved to Josh sitting in the high chair before sliding back to her.

"Settled in okay?"

"Yes, thank you," she said, trying to look busy as she opened a jar of chocolate sprinkles to put on top of the dessert she'd made.

"I see you brought your luggage inside."

She lifted her shoulder. "I needed to unpack."

A few seconds ticked by.

"I'll go shower and clean up before dinner then."

"It'll be ready when you are."

He exited through the kitchen and she concentrated on *not* thinking about Kirk naked in the shower, water spewing off his shoulders and waist. But the image wouldn't budge and the parfaits were well and truly covered with chocolate by the time Josh started to fidget in the high chair.

Her cheeks hot, she lifted her son and carried him down the hallway to put him in his crib. Josh generally settled straight away to sleep and she hoped he would this evening. Her first night here, she didn't want him being too demanding.

She'd already set the table for Kirk in the informal dining room, taking a chance that was where he ate his meals. If he wanted to be served in the more formal dining room then she'd do it his way in the future.

He came to the door as she was checking on the casserole. She caught a glimpse of him dressed in cargo pants and a navy polo shirt. Her pulse skipped a beat.

"Josh gone to bed?"

She closed the door to the wall oven. "Yes. It was a big day for him."

A moment's silence, then, "Where are we eating?"

We?

She looked up and saw him frowning at the table in the far corner of the kitchen where she'd set a place for herself. Surely he didn't want to eat in here with her?

She jerked her head toward the informal dining room. "*You're* eating in there."

His eyes slammed into hers. "You'll be eating with me, of course."

She stiffened. "I'm the housekeeper. I'll eat in here."

"Don't be ridiculous."

She didn't think she was being ridiculous at all. She was just being...cautious.

She lifted her eyebrow. "Did Martha eat her meals with you?"

"No, but I didn't dance with her and kiss her, either."

She gasped. "I don't believe you said that!"

His mouth tightened. "Don't argue, Vanessa. You eat in there with me from now on, or I eat in here with you. Take your pick."

"But...but...this is crazy. You don't even want me working here. Why would you want to eat with me?"

He looked inflexible. "I'm not going to sit in the living room and eat by myself while you sit in here and eat. You and Josh are to join me. End of argument."

He was including Josh in this?

All at once she wondered something. Kirk obviously had plenty of friends in town, and he had plenty of staff on the cattle station, and by the look of his study he was a very busy man there as well. But despite appearances, was he lonely living here in this big house by himself? Did he miss his family? She didn't want to be a family substitute for a man, not even inadvertently. Her own family had already been decimated by the loss of her husband. She couldn't do this again.

Then she looked at the unforgiving look in Kirk's eyes and realized she'd gotten it wrong. This man didn't need her company. He had a full life. He was just determined to make it difficult for her.

Her chin rose as her anger reached its limit. "If you think I'm going to be your whipping boy for the next six months then you have another think coming, *Mr. Deverill*. You either treat me with the respect you afford any employee or I leave tomorrow and I don't care what Linda's reaction will be."

He appeared a little taken aback.

Then he slowly inclined his head with a look of grudging admiration. "You have my word I'll treat you with respect."

She released a breath. "Thank you," she said, recognizing he hadn't forgiven her for thinking she'd used him. He wouldn't forgive her that, but at least now he wouldn't be in her face all the time. "Okay. Now please go in there and I'll bring in the food."

He made a point of grabbing the knife and fork she'd set out for herself. "I'll take these in for you, shall I?"

She nodded. As she watched him leave, she was wondering how she was going to cope eating her meals with him. Her emotions were already being tossed around like clothes in a dryer. Feelings she wanted tucked away nice and neatly in a drawer where no one could see or touch them.

Definitely not Kirk.

Taking a deep breath, she gave him a generous serving of casserole and herself a smaller portion, then took off her apron and smoothed her hands down her skirt. She was glad now that she'd changed into something more formal than jeans.

She groaned inwardly when she saw where she was expected to sit. Kirk had placed her next to him on his right. She'd half hoped he'd put the length of the table between them.

"Everything fine with your rooms?" Kirk said, after she got settled.

"Yes, thank you." She remembered the extra items and she softened toward him. "And thank you for arranging all that baby furniture for Josh. I can't pay you back in one lump sum, but please give me the total amount and I'll make some arrangement to pay by installments."

"Don't worry about it."

"But I don't expect you to supply baby furniture for my son."

"It'll get plenty of use in future," he dismissed, and began eating.

She grasped what he meant. "Oh, of course. If you marry you might use them again."

His face hardened as he swallowed his food before speaking. "No, I meant they can be passed on to someone else in the family eventually."

She picked up her fork. "Oh, I see."

Obviously his future wife wouldn't want secondhand things used by the housekeeper. Grace certainly would never have used anything secondhand, and Nadine would certainly never have to worry about using secondhand furniture, either. Grace wouldn't let her.

"Is there anything else you need?"

"No, the list Martha left was very thorough."

After that they ate their way through dinner while Kirk explained about his routine and more about her duties. At all times his tone was courteous but detached.

Then she brought out the parfaits and tried not to blush at the reason for so many chocolate sprinkles. She *had* gone a bit crazy with them while she'd been thinking about Kirk in the shower.

"You're a good cook," he said after he'd finished eating and placed his spoon in the empty parfait glass.

"I really only made the dessert," she said, hoping any blush in her cheeks would be put down to the compliment and not her wayward thoughts.

"Then I look forward to future meals."

She looked at him to see if he was being sarcastic but his features were calm and controlled.

"By the way, your duties may be more extensive than you thought."

She tensed. Was he going to want bed as well as breakfast?

With a knowing look in his eyes, he placed his napkin on the table and stood up. "Leave the cleaning up for now. I have a surprise for you in the barn."

That got her attention.

She looked up at him suspiciously. "What sort of surprise?"

"It wouldn't be a surprise if I told you," he drawled.

She went with him out the kitchen door and along the path that led to a large barn. She'd seen a couple of horses in the fenced paddock connected to the back of it earlier today, but she was wary of horses and had decided she wouldn't be going near them any time soon.

Just like she was wary of Kirk, she reminded herself, not relaxing until she stepped inside the barn and saw the puppies. They were playing in an area cordoned off so that they couldn't escape.

"Ooh, aren't they're gorgeous?" she said, instinctively falling to her knees to pat their soft fur, forgetting to be guarded with Kirk. "How old are they?"

"About six weeks."

She laughed as the puppies surrounded her and a medium-size dog came trotting up and sniffed her hand. "Is this their mother? Is she some sort of sheep dog?"

A wry smile coated his mouth. "She thinks she is, but no, little Suzi's what we call a 'bitza.' A bit of this and a bit of that." He crouched down and patted the dog's head. "I suspect that's why someone dumped her."

Her heart saddened. "They dumped her? Out here?"

He nodded. "She turned up here one day a few years back, starving and her paws bleeding. She's been with me ever since."

Her assessment of the man went up. She stood and brushed the dirt from her knees. "I guess you need someone to take care of them."

He got to his feet. "If you want to."

"I'd love to," she said sincerely.

He looked almost surprised by her response. "Good. One of my men has been looking after them while I've been away but I'm sure he'll be happy to pass the job to you."

They were standing close and instantly she felt all tingly and aware of his strength. "Er…" She stepped back. "Well, I'd better go clean up the dinner things."

She hurried away without waiting for a response, aware of him watching her. Lord, the attraction was still there between them and if she thought eating together was going to be hard, then how was she going to cope with moments like these?

Right now she didn't have the answer.

Ten minutes later, he walked through the kitchen. "I'll be in the study," he said tersely.

She was relieved. "Do you need anything else?"

His eyes flickered but all he said was, "No. Nothing."

He was remote again and that was fine by her. She wanted it to stay this way. Please God.

She finished cleaning up, then went to her room and watched television before showering and falling into bed. It had been a long day for Josh, but it had been an even longer day for his mother.

Four

At six the next morning, Vanessa stood in the doorway of the kitchen and watched Kirk cooking breakfast at the stove. How was she going to stand looking at *this* every morning? *This* being one male dressed in a khaki shirt and denim jeans who looked more delicious than the breakfast he was making.

As if he sensed he was being watched, he glimpsed over his shoulder, his gaze flicking down over her white top and black jeans. "Good morning," he said, his voice telling her nothing, but his eyes had darkened.

Her nipples instantly tingled and she frowned to cover up her fast-beating heart. "What are you doing?" she asked, taking control of the conversation. Lord knew she had to take control of something.

He turned away to crack an egg into the frying pan. "Cooking breakfast."

"But why are you doing it? I thought that was why I was

here." Pride suddenly made her tense. "I told you before I don't accept charity."

His head shot up. "And I didn't offer it. You're here to run the household, not only the cooking."

She let out a slow breath. Okay, so she'd overreacted a little, but was it any wonder when the man in front of her looked as if he'd been lifted from the cover of a women's magazine.

"You should have left breakfast to me," she felt obligated to say, glad that at least she was going to be of use around here.

"I thought I'd let you settle in on your first morning here."

"Thanks, but I rose ahead of time so I could get things ready for you in case Josh woke early, too."

"No need to do that. I can always wait. Your son can't."

Her heart tilted. She was not sure she wanted to see more of the caring side to Kirk Deverill. She wanted to dislike the man. "I would think—"

"Then don't. If I need to have breakfast early in future and you're not around, then I'll make it myself."

"You shouldn't have to."

He slanted her a sardonic glance. "I think I can manage to feed myself occasionally."

Fine. Who was she to tell him what to do?

"By the way, there's no need for you to feed Suzi this morning. I've already done it. You can start tonight." He began transferring the bacon onto a plate. "Take a seat. Breakfast is ready."

She looked across at the bacon and eggs, then up at the man himself. For a moment she was distracted again by the look of him. "I think I hear Josh," she said, spinning away.

She hurried down the hallway. She hadn't heard Josh at all, but she needed time to get used to sharing breakfast alone with an attractive man other than her husband.

Of course, she had to remember Mike had often been doing shift work and hadn't been home for breakfast, though that wasn't the point. Not being used to intimacy with another man was the main thing here.

Josh was just waking up as she tiptoed over to his crib. She gave him a big good-morning kiss and proceeded to change his diaper and dress him, and by the time she headed back to the kitchen she heard Kirk's vehicle leaving.

Relieved yet anxious to start with her duties, she nevertheless took her time to have a little breakfast with her son. Now *he* was one man she didn't mind sharing breakfast with. Afterward she took him to see the puppies.

Back inside, she started on the housework, carrying him around with her wherever she went and letting him play on the floor where she could keep an eye on him. Eventually she could no longer put off going into Kirk's bedroom. The scent in the air was pleasant and she felt odd entering this masculine domain, as if she were stepping closer to the man himself.

She didn't linger. He was fairly tidy, so she had to only make his bed and straighten up the bathroom. She was actually quite amused to see the damp towel on the bathroom floor. It made him appear more human somehow.

Midmorning she heard a vehicle drive up and when she looked it was Kirk. She was thankful she hadn't still been cleaning his room. In some way it would have made it seem more personal.

"Would you like some cake and coffee?" she asked as he came through the door.

"No, I've just had some." He didn't say where but she figured it was with his men. "Is Josh still awake?"

"Yes. Why?"

"I've got to check something and I thought I'd give you a small tour of the place at the same time."

She hid her surprise. He wasn't being overly friendly but all the same she was glad he'd thought to ask her. "That would be lovely."

"It won't be the full tour but we could still be a couple of hours by the time we visit the cattle yards. You might want to bring along whatever you need for Josh, and something cold for us to drink in case we're longer than I plan." He headed for his study. "I've got to make a few calls first. Let me know when you're ready."

It wasn't too long before they were all off and driving in his Range Rover. The windows were tinted for protection from the sun and the air-conditioning inside the cabin made it a comfortable ride as he drove along a well-worn gravel road. It took Josh a nanosecond to fall asleep in the child's seat in the back.

A few miles farther and he turned off onto a smaller road. The drought was obvious out here, the area sun-baked and parched, with only the gum trees and their gray-green leaves giving any hint of color.

"Where are we going?" she asked, when it looked as if they were just driving for the sake of driving, though she knew that wasn't the case.

"I want to check one of the fences."

In the distance ahead, heat ribboned across the road. "How large is the cattle station?"

"Let's just say it would take us a couple of hours to drive around the boundary."

She was impressed. "That's pretty big."

"My great-grandfather settled out here a long time ago. Deverills have been breeding cattle here ever since," he said with a touch of pride in his voice.

She stole a look at his profile, so strong and dynamic like the man himself. Then he sent her a fleeting look and she quickly focused back on the road ahead. "I can see how easy it would be to become lost out here."

"If you stick to the roads it will lead you somewhere eventually."

She gave a delicate snort. "The roads? You mean these dirt tracks?"

He actually smiled. "Around here, if you drive on it, then it's a road."

She smiled back and she saw his eyes drop to her mouth. The air thickened between them. Then he returned to his driving and she returned to looking out the window, her heart thumping. She knew his look hadn't been deliberate and that made it all the more unsettling.

Farther on they came to a gate across the road and Kirk slowed the vehicle then stopped in front of it, letting the engine run. Vanessa sat there, too, wondering what he was going to do next. Perhaps it was automated?

He turned his head to face her. "It's the passenger's job to hop out and open the gate."

She was startled. "It is?"

"It's customary, yes."

Oh, yes, she remembered hearing about the outback custom now, but had never experienced it.

"It's easy enough to do," he said. "Just unhook the chain and you can swing the gate open."

"Okay." She did as he said, aware he was watching her. Those eyes sent a trickle of sweat running down between her breasts but she ignored it as she hopped back in the vehicle.

He drove forward and stopped. "Now you have to close it," he said, his lips twitching.

She didn't find it funny. "Why didn't you say so before?"

"You didn't ask."

She shot him a withering glance, then got out of the

vehicle, closed the gate, then got back in. She had no problem with opening and shutting the gate, but the rest of it was an unnecessary effort. He could have at least told her instead of letting her look a fool.

"Lighten up, Vanessa," he said, after they'd been driving a minute or so.

"*Me* lighten up? You're the one who—"

"Bloody hell!" Unexpectedly he turned the wheel and drove off the road and onto the dried grass. It became clear he was heading for a portion of a broken fence. "I knew it. Brady was supposed to fix this yesterday." He didn't look pleased as he stopped the vehicle beneath a tree. "He'll have to go."

She was relieved *she* wasn't the object of his anger but she felt a little sorry for this Brady. "Perhaps he didn't have enough time?"

"Then he could bloody well make time," he snapped, then expelled a breath. "This isn't the first time he hasn't followed orders. He was given a second chance and now he's lied to my farm manager. That's it as far as I'm concerned."

She could understand that, but still she couldn't help but feel sorry for the other man. Kirk would be a hard taskmaster. He didn't like being let down. *She* knew that more than anyone.

He opened his door and climbed out of the vehicle. "You can get out and stretch your legs, if you like." Then he peeked over the back at a sleeping Josh. "It's going to get hot in here with the engine off, but I can't keep the air-con running for too long even with the engine on. It'll be best if you open all the doors to give him some breeze. I'll try not to be too long, but let me know if he starts stressing and we'll head back."

Vanessa did as suggested and opened all the doors while he retrieved a toolbox from the back. He may be hard on others but she couldn't fault his thoughtfulness in regards to her son. He certainly showed a very human side when it came to Josh.

Unlike the side he showed her.

No, she wouldn't think that right now. Kirk was kind enough to bring her on this outing when he'd had no need, especially as he didn't want her as his housekeeper in the first place.

It was enough.

The quiet must have woken Josh because he opened his eyes. Chatting to him, she poured some water on a cloth and wiped his face to keep him cool, then unbuckled him and gave him a bottle of juice. She stood under the tree and watched Kirk fix the fence, Josh on her hip.

"How's he doing?" Kirk asked after a few minutes.

"He's okay."

"I'm almost done here. We'll soon have him cool."

His genuine interest in her son's well-being took her by surprise again, but not for the first time since Mike's death she wondered about Josh not having a father. As a child she'd taught herself not to miss having a dad, but would her son? Her childhood had been difficult at times when so many of the other kids seemed to have a father. Would Josh feel cheated because he didn't have a man to show him all the things that fathers should? Or because he didn't have a father who could come to the school play or a church picnic? A father to complete the family?

Her thoughts too painful, she pushed her sadness away.

Just then Kirk reached forward to pick up one of the tools from the box, and her gaze lowered to the open neck of his khaki shirt where she could see a light sprinkling of chest hair. All at once her hands itched to slide through the wisps of dark hair and curl her fingers into him. Quickly she looked away.

"Finished," he said after a few more minutes, then dropped the tools back in the box and came toward her. "Ready for the rest of the tour?"

She nodded. She was more than ready to move on.

Soon they were on their way again, heading back the way they'd come—at least she *thought* they were—then taking a detour. She had to open and close a couple of gates but soon they seemed to be coming back toward civilization.

"That paddock over there is a cropping paddock," he pointed out as they drove.

"There's nothing in it. Is that because of the drought?"

"No. It's just been sprayed, that's all. That way it can be ready to plant crops in a few months' time."

"What sort of crops?"

"Cereals. Things like wheat, which we sell, and barley and oats for cattle feed."

Then he went on to show her all the different types of paddocks from calf paddocks to weaner paddocks, breeding cow paddocks to bull paddocks. There were so many paddocks her head spun. And they weren't tiny little parcels of land, either. They stretched for miles and miles.

"Naturally I keep my best stud cows in a separate paddock closer to the yards."

"Of course." She understood these animals cost thousands of dollars. He'd have them where his men could keep a close eye on them.

Finally they drove up to the cattle yards. Beyond were huge sheds that Kirk said stored feed and fertilizer and machinery, and farther beyond were the manager's residence and the workmen's cottages.

One of the men rushed to open the gate for them and Vanessa smiled to herself. She never thought someone opening a gate would be such a big thing, yet she felt like a queen.

She was soon introduced to some of the staff. She could imagine her presence as housekeeper was making the rounds of gossip, but they were all very polite and pleasant and some of the men even seemed shy.

Then she was introduced to the farm manager, but not before she heard Kirk ask him about Brady's whereabouts and learned that Tom had fired the man over a dispute earlier. Brady apparently had already cleared out.

"Good," Kirk said, looking grimly satisfied.

Before long the farm manager's wife, Fay, hurried over to introduce herself. She was a pleasant woman in her forties who insisted they come to the house for lunch.

"Thanks, Fay," Kirk said, "but one of the trucks has arrived early to pick up a load of stock for sale. Tom and I have to help." He looked at Vanessa. "I'm sure Vanessa would be happy to keep you company."

"I'd love to," Vanessa said.

She and Josh ended up staying a couple of hours, and she learned that Fay was Kirk's office manager and helped out a lot with the bookwork.

"I can do a lot from here," Fay said, showing Vanessa her office, complete with the latest computer equipment. "And twice a week I pop up to the main house to do things like filing or collecting the letters for the post that I've e-mailed Kirk and he's signed." Fay smiled. "But I always made time for coffee and a chat with Martha."

"Well, I hope you'll make time for the same with me."

Fay's smiled widened. "That would be lovely."

After that, Kirk drove Vanessa and Josh back to the homestead. "What do you think of Fay?" he asked, once he'd parked the Range Rover near the front steps. "You seemed to get on well together."

Her face relaxed. "She's really nice."

He nodded, then, "And what do you think of Deverill Downs?"

She had the feeling he cared what she thought. "It has a certain charm," she said, and meant it, then recognized that this really wasn't about *her.* This was about the pride he had for his cattle station.

He looked pleased and that was that.

The next morning, Vanessa had put Josh down for his morning nap when she heard Suzi barking out in the barn. She didn't want to think about snakes, though it definitely crossed her mind as she made her way outside.

She found Suzi over in the corner, barking at something beneath a large wooden bench. Heart thumping, Vanessa took a quick look back at the knee-high partition erected around the pups. She counted them and realized one was missing, then saw a small hole at one corner of the wood where it must have escaped.

Grabbing the flashlight hanging near the door, she shone it under the bench. And there was a sleeping puppy. Suzi hadn't been able to get to her offspring because a roll of wire partially blocked it.

She turned to Suzi. "So you think we should get him out, huh?"

Suzi sat looking at her expectantly.

"Okay, little mother. Give me a moment."

Trying not to think about spiders and snakes and every other poisonous animal that seemed to inhabit this country, Vanessa reached under the bench and drew the puppy toward her.

"Here we go," she said, placing it in front of Suzi, who barked then picked it up in her teeth and trotted back to the others.

Smiling, Vanessa pushed herself to her feet. But as she went to stand, she heard a ripping noise and felt a pain at the back of her left shoulder blade. She gasped. Had she just been bitten by a snake? She glanced behind her and went weak with relief when she saw a nail sticking out of the bench.

Reaching over her shoulder, she managed to touch the gash. Her fingers came away with blood on them. Great. That was all she needed. Stitches.

Looking in the bathroom mirror a few minutes later, she was thankful to see a cut only about half an inch long and not too deep. A bit painful but nothing she couldn't handle, she decided, dabbing at it with antiseptic cream from the first-aid kit in the laundry room, then changing into another blouse.

It hurt like the devil as she went back to the kitchen but she ignored the pain as best she could. She'd just decided to gather the ingredients to make a lemon meringue pie for dessert when she heard the sound of Kirk's vehicle returning.

Her pulse started to race and she called herself a fool for letting him affect her this way. He was her employer, for heaven's sake. He had come home for lunch, that was all. He hadn't come home to see *her*.

Vanessa reminded herself that she still had to be wary where Kirk was concerned. Attraction, that was all it was. She'd been without her husband for a while, and Kirk was used to having any woman he wanted.

She heard him come in the back door and stop to wash his hands in the laundry, then his footsteps came to the kitchen door. She pretended to be busy wiping the sink down.

A moment crept by.

She knew he was there.

She started to casually turn and—

"Bloody hell, Vanessa." He strode toward her. "You've got blood on the back of your blouse. What happened?"

She whirled around and found Kirk far too close for comfort. Alarm flashed through her.

She swallowed. "One of the pups escaped and I got caught on a nail getting him out from under the bench."

"Let me take a look."

She stepped back but came up against the sink. "No, I cleaned it up myself and put some antiseptic cream on it. And I had a tetanus shot last year when I walked on a nail, so you don't have to worry about that."

Kirk ignored her as he turned her around, holding her still. "It's been bleeding. Now it's stuck to your shirt. I'd better take a proper look at it."

She went to move away. "It's nothing. Really."

"You may need stitches."

"I don't."

He paid no attention as he strode toward the laundry room. "I'll get the first-aid kit. We'll use the guest bathroom. It's got good light in there." He disappeared, then came back with the small box in his hand. "Come on, Vanessa. Don't dilly-dally. You don't want to risk it getting infected."

There was nothing for it but to follow him along the hallway to the guest bathroom.

He placed a stool in front of the basin. "Sit."

She sat but she was getting annoyed at his bossy attitude. "Want me to roll over, too?"

His gaze snapped to hers in the mirror. "I generally save that for the bedroom," he said, with a smirk.

"You wish!"

A glint returned to his eyes before he pulled out a wad of cotton wool from the first-aid kit. "Right. It's going to hurt like hell, but if I wet it first the material should come off easily." He paused at their reflection, his eyes plunging to her blouse then up again. "You know you'll have to take that off afterward, don't you?"

All at once the air charged with electricity. It zipped between them, alive and determined to be recognized.

Panic rose in her throat. Her eyes darted to the box of

assorted items. "Didn't I see a pair of scissors in there? Just cut around it. I don't mind."

His movements stiff, he turned the faucet on and held the cotton wool under running water. "You'll ruin another shirt," he warned.

She shrugged. "What's one more?"

Not looking at her, he placed the water-soaked gauze on the cut and dabbed at it a few times, causing her to flinch. "Sorry, I'm being as gentle as I can."

She swallowed. "I know."

"There." Another second or two and he lifted the cotton wool away. "You should be able to take the blouse off now without too much damage."

Her breathing shallowed.

His eyes caught and held hers, and suddenly she was imagining having his strong arms around her, his warm kisses.

"Want some help?" he said, his voice thickening, a pulse ticking in the strong cord of his neck.

She could feel herself blush. "Er…no. I can manage." She willed her hands to move, only they wouldn't.

A few seconds went by.

"Sure?"

"Yes. I mean, no."

The blue of his eyes darkened like a midnight sky. "Can't make up your mind?" he asked huskily.

"No. I mean, yes."

He made a guttural sound, his expression stilling. All at once there was nothing more serious than this moment. Nothing more serious than *them*.

She watched, mesmerized in the mirror, as his hand came to rest on her good shoulder…rested then tiptoed along her collarbone to her throat.

She moistened her lips. "Er…what are you doing?"

His blue eyes said it all. "I don't know," he muttered. "I just don't bloody know."

Her heartbeat slammed against her ribs. She had to bring back some sense of sanity. "Don't touch, remember?" she tried to remind him, tried to take charge, only her voice merely dropped into the whirlpool of sensuality in the room.

"I remember. But…if I *were* to touch I'd do it like…" His index finger touched the sensitive hollows of her neck. "This."

She moaned silently, her breath entering her lungs in short spurts.

His finger slipped inside the collar of her blouse. "And touching's not always the same as…caressing." He stroked the top of one breast.

Oh, God.

"It's not?"

"No. There's a difference." Another pass over the top of her breast. "Feel it?"

She moistened her lips. She could feel nothing else. Closing her eyes, she gave in for a moment, all soft and pliable and very much a woman. "Oh, yes."

And he was very much a man.

An *aroused* man. She only had to turn her head and she'd be able to press her cheek against him, inhale him and—

Her eyes burst open and she jumped to her feet, shaken by how easily things had gotten out of control. "Um…it'll be okay. Don't worry about the cut. It won't get infected. I know it won't. It—"

His face closed up. The moment had passed. "Sit down, Vanessa."

She shook her head. "No. It'll be fine, you'll see." She leaped the distance to the open doorway.

"Vanessa?"

She turned. "Look, it's okay. I'll just stick a plaster over it or something."

His eyes pierced the distance between them. "You know, Vanessa, sometimes a plaster isn't enough."

Unable to stand the tension of being cooped up in the house with Vanessa any longer, Kirk ate a quick lunch then took off for the cattle yards to see how his men were going with fixing a broken water pipe. He had to keep busy.

What the hell was he thinking bringing her here to Deverill Downs? Damn him for letting himself be coerced into this. She hadn't fooled him, of course. She may fool herself into believing that using him was acceptable, but any respect he afforded her was only as she wanted—as an employee. And even that was going to be difficult for him at times when every instinct inside him warred between wanting her and trying to keep perspective.

God, she'd looked bloody magnificent when she'd flared up at him though. She was lucky he hadn't swept her up in his arms, carried her to his room and made love to her until dawn.

He'd known it was going to be difficult keeping his hands off her. So the last thing he'd needed today was to apply first aid to her back.

Her lovely, sexy back.

Just the thought of touching her soft skin…of being in a confined space with her…her scent…drove him wild.

He had to stop thinking about it.

He had to stop thinking about *her*.

He even managed to do that during dinner that evening but only because she was right there in front of him and he didn't have to *think*. Not when he could *see* her.

Josh ate dinner with them, and that helped, though Kirk

suspected Vanessa deliberately kept her son up past his bedtime. Not that he minded. He had to admit he was growing to like the kid. Josh had a charm that snuck up on a person.

Like the boy's mother.

Only, Vanessa's charm wasn't pure and innocent like her son's. There was danger in her charms. A man could drown in them. Drown and not even care.

Thankfully tonight there was a lifesaver in the vicinity in the form of Josh. He was a welcome distraction and Kirk couldn't help but be mildly amused at his antics. Every time Vanessa turned away from him to eat her dinner, Josh babbled something and dropped his spoon over the side of the high chair.

Kirk looked at her son and felt something kick him inside. Josh was like the son he would have loved to have had one day.

The son he would *never* have.

He forced away his inner pain. "He's doing that deliberately, you know," he felt obligated to point out as she mildly scolded Josh and gave him a new spoon.

"I know," she said, her mouth curving with tenderness.

Careful, he told himself. "You do?"

"It's a game, Kirk, that's all." Josh babbled and dropped the spoon again and she gave a soft chuckle. "See." She bent to pick it up but this time didn't replace the spoon. "No more, young man. That's enough."

Kirk's brows drew together. All that bending over wasn't good for her back.

Her lovely, sexy back.

The image returned. Both of them in the bathroom. The scent of her… "How's the cut?" he all but growled.

Her safe-and-sound smile faltered and two pink dots appeared in her cheeks. "It's a bit sore," she said, averting her eyes.

Masculine pleasure spurted through him at her reaction.

She might not admit she was attracted to him, but her body couldn't deny the magnetism between them.

"Then keep an eye on it," he said gruffly, and went back to eating.

Straight after dinner he headed to the study, glad to be able to throw himself into his bookwork with renewed determination. He even managed to put thoughts of Vanessa aside and concentrate on the job at hand.

There was always a ton of paperwork to deal with in an operation this size. Fay was a terrific help as an office assistant, and he employed someone in Jackaroo Plains to do his accounts. But there was still a lot to do himself. Filling in government forms and surveys, plus keeping up-to-date with world breeding programs, latest research and development, and long-range weather predictions, took up much of his time.

Around an hour later he remembered he'd left the local newspaper on the hallway table. It had market data on recent sales and stock prices and he'd wanted to read it.

As he headed down the hallway, he heard Vanessa's soft voice in the kitchen.

"I said I'd call you when I could, Grace," she was quietly chiding. "You didn't have to call the motel."

For a minute he thought they had visitors, but then he realized she must be talking on her cell phone.

"No, I wasn't trying to hide anything from you. I just wanted to settle in here first."

Pause.

"There's nothing to be upset about. I was going to stay at Jackaroo Plains for six months anyway. Nothing's really changed."

Another pause.

"What? You've got a dossier on him already? Then you'll know he's a good man."

They were talking about *him*.

"He's rich? So? That's not why I'm here. Money doesn't matter to me. I'm only his temporary housekeeper when all is said and done."

A long silence followed her words.

"Grace, I can't help it if you don't like it. I needed to get away for a while. You know that." All at once, Josh started to cry. "Look, I have to go. Josh needs to go to bed."

Silence.

"Yes, he's up late but he's a bit restless tonight. He might be teething. Yes, call me later in the week."

She hung up.

There was a heavy sigh. "And yes, Grace, I'm peachy-keen, too," she mused out loud.

Kirk didn't bother about the newspaper. He quietly went back to the study and frowned as he sat down at his desk. Okay, so that conversation had substantiated some of what Linda had told him about Vanessa's in-laws. They *had* sounded a trifle overbearing.

But perhaps they were merely concerned for the welfare of their family? That was understandable. He sure as hell would be checking out a person if one of his family were staying with someone he didn't know.

No, he wasn't convinced Vanessa had needed this job.

And that meant she hadn't needed to use *him*.

Five

Vanessa wasn't sure how she managed to fall asleep that night. She kept seeing images of Kirk's fingers sliding over the top of her breasts, interspersed with images of her outraged in-laws. Either way she was in trouble. Kirk wasn't supposed to "touch" her, and she wasn't supposed to let him, and neither of them wanted any type of intimate relations. And then there was Grace and Rupert. Her in-laws had not been happy after telephoning the motel, only to be told by one of the staff that Vanessa and Josh had moved to Deverill Downs.

So she should have expected to see them getting out of the rental car just after ten. She was vacuuming at the time and hadn't heard the car drive up.

At least Kirk wasn't here to witness any of this. She could only hope they would be gone by the time he came home for lunch.

Pushing open the screen door, she stepped onto the verandah as they marched up the steps. "This *is* a surprise," she said with a smile that took all her control.

And then some.

Grace gave her a quick peck on the cheek, but her eyes were cold. "We wanted to come and see Joshua."

"Of course."

Rupert kissed her cheek next. "We haven't seen the boy since Christmas."

The boy.

Vanessa gritted her teeth. "The boy" had a name. And while it might seem a lot of time since Christmas to her in-laws, it wasn't near enough time for Vanessa. All those phone calls had made it seem far less than five weeks ago.

"Did you have much trouble finding us?" she asked, hoping Grace didn't hear the hint of sarcasm in her voice. She had to stay composed. She didn't want any more trouble than expected from them.

"A little," her mother-in-law said, brushing a speck of fluff off her expensive pantsuit. She looked up and gave a false smile. "But that won't stop us seeing our grandson." Her smile didn't reach her eyes.

Rupert rubbed his hands together. "Where is he?"

Vanessa's gaze shot to her father-in-law. "Who?"

"Joshua, of course."

"Oh, yes." She kept her face blank, not giving anything away. For a minute there she'd thought he meant Kirk. "He's taking his morning nap."

"Then wake him up and let us see the boy," Rupert said. "We've come a long way."

Vanessa held on to her temper. "Let's have a cool drink first. Josh should be awake by then." She pointed to the wicker chairs along the verandah. "Take a seat, relax and look at the view."

They hesitated but for once she stood her ground until they were seated, then she went to get the drinks. She didn't want them inside and today wasn't too hot to sit outside, thank goodness. As it was, she kept an ear out in case they decided to enter the house. She didn't trust them not to look for Josh and wake him up, leaving him cranky long after they left.

If they left.

The thought filled her with anxiety. She certainly hoped they didn't expect to stay here overnight. She would definitely have to put her foot down if they did. She was only the housekeeper here and she could imagine Kirk's response.

She carried the tray out to them. "So. What do you think of the place?" she chatted. "It's lovely, isn't it? I hope it's put your mind at rest about Josh and myself moving here."

"That's only temporary, dear," Grace clarified, then surveyed the area with a critical eye. "Yes, it's nice but far too isolated. What if Joshua came down with something? What if you needed a doctor?"

"Then we'd call one to come out here or go into town. We're not that far from civilization." She began pouring the iced tea. "Are you staying in the area long? I suppose you've already booked into a motel."

For the life of her she couldn't imagine them staying at Linda and Hugh's motel. They would prefer one of the larger ones in Dubbo.

"We came straight from Dubbo Airport and haven't booked in anywhere yet. We thought we might—" Grace broke off as Vanessa handed her the glass. "Oh, my God, you're not wearing your rings. What happened to them, Vanessa? Have you lost them?"

Vanessa hid her wince. Trust her mother-in-law to spot that straightaway and make it sound as if it was the crime of the century.

"No, I've put them in a safe place. They were too tight out here in this heat, that's all. I didn't want to get them adjusted, so I decided to take them off until I go back to Sydney."

Mollified, Grace accepted the explanation. "Yes, everything should return to normal once you're back home."

Vanessa looked down at her drink. Was Sydney home anymore? She wasn't so sure.

"Someone's coming."

Vanessa heard her father-in-law's words and her head snapped up. She groaned inwardly. Kirk's Range Rover could be seen driving toward the house.

"That's my employer," she said brightly. Heaven help her. Grace would spot the tension between them at fifty paces.

"Good. I want to meet this Kirk Deverill," Rupert said, a self-important quality in his voice.

"Why?" Vanessa's brightness dimmed, her back up now. She couldn't help it.

"Our grandson is living in his house."

Was Rupert insulting Kirk? It certainly sounded like it. And it was one thing for *her* to think bad of Kirk. It was another for these two people to consider Kirk some sort of villain when they hadn't even met him.

"I think we have that right," Grace added.

Vanessa silently choked. These two people had little rights where Josh was concerned. Yes, they had rights as grandparents to concern themselves with their grandchild's well-being. But more than that and any further "right" with them was totally *wrong*.

"I believe you'll find both Josh and I are in safe hands with Kirk."

Grace shot her a sharp look as the vehicle drew to a halt behind the rental car. "You call your employer by his first name?"

Grace would have a fit if she knew that Kirk had kissed her daughter-in-law, that he'd touched her breasts. "They're very friendly out here."

Her mother-in-law clicked her tongue. "It would never do in the city, Vanessa. Remember that when you come back home."

There it was again. Did Grace have to keep mentioning about going back home? Her in-laws had no idea what a true home should be like. Mike had known that and he'd often ignored their antics, but in the long run they'd still been his parents.

She remained in her chair as Kirk came up the steps, carrying his hat. Better not to let any of them know how anxious she felt. "Kirk, I hope you don't mind, but my parents-in-law have come to visit," she said, then introduced them.

He inclined his head at the older couple. "Not at all." He didn't glance her way and for that she was grateful. "You've come a long way."

"We thought it our responsibility to come and check things out," Rupert said, without quite the haughty tone he'd used before. Clearly Rupert recognized a potential enemy.

"We wanted to see our grandson," Grace added.

"And Vanessa, too, no doubt."

Grace's lips pursed. "Of course."

Kirk considered them, his eyes unreadable. "Vanessa has been a real help to me after my housekeeper had to leave suddenly."

"Yes, it's so hard to get good help at times," Grace commiserated.

Kirk stiffened, and Vanessa jumped to her feet. "What am I thinking?" she exclaimed, knowing Kirk was fully aware Grace had insulted her. "I'll go make you some morning tea. Or perhaps you'd like lunch early? There's some salad and—"

"I'll get something later," he cut across her, a determined jut to his chin. He turned back to the other pair and stood looking down at them. "So you think—"

A small cry came from inside the house.

"Oh, I think I hear Joshua now," Grace exclaimed, her eyes lighting up in a way reserved only for her grandson. She went to get to her feet. "I'll go get him."

"No. I'll get him." Kirk strode to the door and disappeared inside, not giving the older woman a chance to reply.

Grace fell back in her chair and looked at Vanessa, her mouth tightening. "He seems very…protective of Joshua, dear."

Vanessa went and sat back down again. "He was just being nice," she said and got a slightly skeptical look from her mother-in-law. Quickly she changed the subject. "So tell me about Nadine."

That subject was obviously more to Grace's taste and she launched into an enthusiastic reply, more enthusiastic than Vanessa had seen her in a long time. By the time Kirk came back carrying a sleepy-eyed Josh, Vanessa was more than hopeful Grace would focus on Nadine's baby once it was born, leaving her and Josh to get on with their lives in relative peace.

Her mother-in-law got to her feet and hurried toward the pair. "Oh, give him to me."

Josh let out a startled cry and wrapped his arms around Kirk's neck, hiding his face and holding on for dear life, as if he didn't remember his grandmother and she frightened him. Vanessa saw Kirk's arms tighten around her son.

"Now come on, Joshua," Grace chided. The small boy didn't move and she looked at Kirk as if it was his fault. "Right, Mr. Deverill. I'll take him now."

Vanessa saw the pulse beat in Kirk's neck but before she could react, Grace had practically dragged Josh out of his arms and was carrying her startled grandson back to her chair.

"There we go," Grace said, sitting him on her lap. She looked at them all with a triumphant smile. "See. You shouldn't let him dictate to you. You're the adult. He's the child." Her gaze returned to her grandson. "You know, I don't think he's grown at all," she said, with a disapproving eye. "What do you think, Rupert?"

Rupert cast his eyes over his grandson. "I think you're right, Grace."

Grace's gaze slid to Vanessa. "I'm sure he should be growing much faster than he is. Are you feeding him enough, Vanessa?"

Vanessa gritted her teeth. Josh was thriving. Her mother-in-law was merely looking for an excuse to criticize her. "Grace, I can assure you that Josh has grown and put on weight."

The older woman looked at her grandson with another frown that quickly disappeared when Josh's bottom lip started to drop. "Now none of that, young man," she scolded.

Vanessa saw Josh's bottom lip tremble and she jumped to her feet. "He probably just needs his diaper changed," she said, scooping him out of Grace's arms, every motherly instinct on high alert. "I'll take him inside and change him, then I'll bring him back."

Grace looked as if she was about to follow, but Kirk surprised Vanessa by stepping forward. "So, Grace," he said, sitting down on the chair Vanessa had vacated. "How did you get here?" he asked, almost conversationally. "Did you drive or fly?"

Grace blinked, then appeared to focus. "Oh, we flew to Dubbo, didn't we, Rupert?"

Vanessa left them to it. It was a pity Josh's diaper hadn't soaked through to Grace's pantsuit, she mused, though no doubt Grace would have forgiven him.

And blamed *her*.

And why had Kirk attracted Grace's attention right now like that? It was as though he'd thrown himself on a live grenade to protect her and Josh. Her heart quickened. Did it mean he was recognizing she had a valid reason for not returning to Sydney? She hadn't mentioned her in-laws to him, but he'd been around when Linda had mentioned them and her cousin was sure to have filled him in on the details. So this would have more to do with shielding Josh from his grandparents than anything to do with *her.*

And for that she would be forever grateful.

It took her ten minutes to change Josh's diaper then head to the kitchen to heat up a bottle of formula. She also set the table for one and quickly put together a plate of salad and cold meats and left it in the refrigerator in case Kirk wanted an early lunch.

"Here we are," she said, stepping out onto the verandah carrying Josh and the bottle of formula.

"Oh, let me feed him," Grace said, practically snatching the bottle from Vanessa's hand.

Vanessa knew she didn't have a chance in hell of not letting her mother-in-law give Josh his bottle, so she handed Josh over. Thankfully he was hungry and too busy drinking to cry.

Then Vanessa gave Kirk a brief smile. "I'll let you go inside now, Kirk. Thank you so much for looking after Grace and Rupert for me while I took care of Josh." She was aware she was dismissing her boss but she needed to get at least one tension-filled person out of the area.

Kirk's eyes flickered then he pushed to his feet. "It was nice meeting you both. Have a safe trip back." He went inside without waiting for a response, a commanding air about him that said he was in charge and no one would take that away from him.

"I don't think he's very happy with you, dear," Grace said, a slightly gleeful note to her voice.

Vanessa shrugged. "He'll get over it."

"You really shouldn't talk like that to your employer. He might fire you." Grace's eyes took on a bright sheen. "If he does, make sure you let us know and we'll come straight here and take you home. It won't be a bother."

"I'm sure."

After that, things settled down and the visit was almost pleasant. Vanessa didn't encourage them to stay longer—she was an employee here after all—and an hour later they left rather reluctantly, with a promise from Vanessa that she would call them tomorrow. She sighed.

Kirk waited until he heard the car leave before he came out of his study. He had no wish to see Vanessa's in-laws again. He'd been wrong in thinking they were only a *little* overbearing. Grace was the type to choke the life out of a person, and Rupert a pompous ass. He hadn't needed to hear them open their mouths to know that. One look at them had said it all.

So could he really blame Vanessa for scheming to get her son out from under their influence?

No, he couldn't.

Could he still blame her for using *him* to do it?

Yes, he could.

She'd had a month to arrange something, and there were other ways she could have approached all this. If she'd been aboveboard he could have helped her find lodgings and a suitable job. Yet once she'd done working on her cousin, this job had been the *only* position Linda would accept. And Linda would never have forgiven him for not giving Vanessa that option.

So why did he feel more kindly toward her now? He didn't want to, but dammit, anyone connected to that older couple deserved sympathy, he decided, as he opened the screen door and went out on the verandah.

"You could have invited them to lunch," he said, watching her come up the steps carrying Josh. She looked...despondent.

Something clutched inside him.

She reached the top step. "No. It's not my place." Her nose wrinkled. "I mean, it's not my place as housekeeper to invite my relatives into your home."

"If you'd wanted to invite them inside then you could have."

"Oh." Her face softened. "Well, thank you." Then she paused. "By the way, I apologize if it looked like I was dismissing you in front of them. I didn't want you to feel obligated to spend time with us."

He'd known what she was doing. "I appreciate that."

She blinked. "Really? I thought..."

"What?"

"You looked angry."

"I *was* angry." The feeling ignited again. "At them." He hadn't liked the way Grace had either ignored Vanessa or put her down.

She looked pleased then slightly embarrassed. "They're a bit overpowering at first."

"You could say that," he derided. She had nothing to be embarrassed about. It was her in-laws who should be embarrassed.

And right now they needed to clear their minds of her relatives. "Come on. We're going for a walk." He reached inside the screen door to grab two hats off the hat pegs. "We need some exercise."

"Exercise?"

"We need to stretch our legs. We can show Josh the horses."

"H-horses?"

He handed her his sister's hat. "You can use this. It

belongs to Jade." He looked at Josh's fair skin. "Have you got a hat for Josh?"

"Er...yes."

"Put some sunscreen on, as well. Yourself, too. We won't be out in the sun very long but I don't want either of you getting sunburned." He held the screen door open for her to pass. "I'll meet you back here in five minutes."

She stood there for a moment, looking uncertain.

"Something the matter?"

"Um...no." She stepped into the house. "I won't be long."

He watched her walk down the hallway, her jeans caressing her backside and long legs, closer to her skin than a man's hand. The brief thought of spreading the sunscreen's creamy lotion over Vanessa's soft skin sent the blood surging to his groin.

It was about ten minutes before she came back with Jade's Akubra hat now on her head. It looked good on her. "Feel free to use that whenever you need to."

"Thanks."

Then his gaze slid to Josh. The kid looked cute in shorts, a T-shirt and a sunhat, with sunblock smeared over any bare skin. A band of inner pain tightened around Kirk's chest.

He saw her adjust Josh on her hip. "Here, let me take him for you," he said brusquely, and lifted Josh out of her arms. The infant was getting too heavy for her to carry around for any length of time.

Aware of Josh holding on to his neck, Kirk felt a tug on his heartstrings as he went down the steps. Vanessa walked with him and they followed the driveway around the side of the house toward the paddock behind the barn.

"Your sister's name is Jade, isn't it?" she chatted, as if nervous. "It's a pretty name."

He sent her a momentary look, not sure why she would be

feeling nervous. He wasn't about to make a move on her, especially with her son here with them.

And not even if Josh *wasn't* here with them.

He grimaced and got back to the question. "Jade doesn't think so. She says it makes her sound like she's jaded."

"And is she? Jaded, that is."

"Sometimes." His mouth tightened as he remembered his sister's last boyfriend who had hit her once and only once. If Jade hadn't charged him with assault, then *he* would have.

"What does she do for a living?"

"She's in public relations for a multimedia company in Sydney. She's doing very well. Even has her own place overlooking the harbor." Kirk pulled his head back out of reach as Josh tried to grab the brim of his hat. The kid was fast.

"Does your mother live with her?" Vanessa asked.

He gave a short laugh. "Not in this lifetime."

Her fine eyebrows shot up in surprise. "They don't get on?"

"Actually they do, but not if they live together. Doesn't stop Mum from keeping an eye on her though."

"Jade must be thrilled," Vanessa said with a touch of cynicism that told Kirk immediately what she was thinking.

"My mother isn't like Grace, Vanessa. Mum knows how to let her children breathe."

"You're lucky."

He was in that respect. He had even suspected his mother had known he was getting serious about Samantha and that was why she had moved to Sydney after his father's death, leaving the cattle station open for him to bring home a wife. Getting his mother to admit it was more than not wanting to live here without his father was another thing.

He scowled at the reminder of Samantha. The woman didn't deserve a moment more of his thoughts.

"You have a brother, too, don't you?" Vanessa continued the conversation. "I saw a photo in the main bedroom of you and another man when you were teenagers. You were with a young girl whom I assume was Jade."

He felt his face close up. He remembered that photograph. "Zach's a couple of years younger than me and a year older than Jade. He lives in Queensland." Enough about that. "What about you? Any brothers or sisters?"

She missed a step, then shook her head. "No. Just me."

"Parents?"

"Two, actually."

His mouth quirked. "Are they still alive?"

"My father died when I was little and my mother remarried five years ago and went to live in England."

"Are you close?"

She hesitated. "Not really. We love each other but we've never really been on the same wavelength. I'm much closer to Linda. Her mother and mine were sisters, you know, except Aunt Emily had five children and mine…well, she only had me." She gave a strained smile. "Linda says she's going to have six children just to outdo her mother."

"And you?" he heard himself asking. "Do you want to outdo your mother?"

She stuck her hands in her jean pockets. "I did want a big family but…" Her shoulders hunched. "Who knows now?"

A chill washed over him. It was clear she didn't want to discuss it and neither should he. Talking about having children wasn't his favorite topic. Now more than ever it was important he not scale the boundaries he'd set between them.

They came up to the paddock railing. Time to put the discussion to rest, he decided, whistling softly to the two horses grazing under a tree, not surprised when only one of them started to trot toward him.

Without warning, Vanessa gripped his arm and didn't let go. "Kirk, please don't let Josh too close to the horses."

It only took a second to comprehend the reason for her earlier nervousness. It wasn't because of being around him. It was because of the horses. His ego would have taken a dive if the touch of her hand on his arm wasn't rushing through him. If she only knew what she was doing to his pulse, she might realize she had her priorities wrong.

"You're scared of horses, aren't you?"

She looked a little self-conscious. "I'm a city girl. I haven't been around them much."

"You can give me my arm back now," he drawled, trying to lighten the moment. He wasn't totally without understanding.

She dropped her hand away, a blush creeping into her cheeks. "Um…sorry."

He was sorrier that he couldn't allow her to keep touching him. "If it makes you feel better, then you should hold Josh." He returned her son to her, watching as she hastily took a step back when Sabre reached the railing.

Kirk reached out to stroke the bay's head. "Hey, fella. How you doing? Enjoying your retirement?" This one had been his father's. "This is Sabre," he said in a reassuring tone. "He's a friendly chap. Now Sadie over there prefers to keep her distance."

Vanessa's gaze darted across the paddock then back. "Do you ride them?" Josh squirmed then to get out of her arms, but she held on tight.

"Not now they're old. They belonged to my parents." Sabre nudged his hand and he gave a low laugh. "Okay, boy, I know. You want some sugar."

Josh babbled something unintelligible and Kirk smiled. "That's right, Josh. He's pushy." Taking some sugar cubes out of his shirt pocket that he'd taken from the kitchen, Kirk put them in Sabre's mouth and watched him scoff them down.

The horse nudged him again. "No more, boy." Another nudge. "Okay, okay. You're waiting for an introduction, aren't you?" He patted the horse's neck. "This is Vanessa and Josh. They're staying here awhile, so you'll see them about the place."

Sabre stood watching Vanessa and Josh, and Kirk let him get used to them. The horse seemed to sense that he needed to stand quietly.

"Come closer and let him sniff your hand. He wants to smell you."

She shook her head. "He looks like he wants to eat me."

He wasn't the only one, he mused.

"Sabre doesn't bite. He's as gentle as a lamb these days."

Her eyes widened. "These days?"

"He was my father's horse so you can't expect him not to have been young and frisky at one time. He would never have bitten anyone that he liked anyway." He paused a few seconds. "He likes you and Josh. I can tell."

She blinked. "You can?"

He nodded. "He's almost purring at you."

Her face started to relax but right then Sabre tossed his head and she jumped. "Oh!"

Kirk had to smile. "He's only getting rid of a fly."

"He startled me."

"He didn't mean to. Look, he wants you to pat him."

She contemplated the horse again. "I guess he does have nice eyes," she eventually admitted. "Sort of big and velvety. Like Bambi."

"Bambi! Don't let him hear you say that. He's got his pride, you know." She gave a rueful smile and he held out his hand. "Come on. Move in closer."

Her smile disappeared. "But Josh—"

"I won't let either of you get hurt."

She hesitated, then did as he asked but he noticed she half turned so that Josh was farthest away from the bay.

"Now hold your hand out so he can sniff you." She carefully did what he suggested. "That's it," he encouraged, as Sabre stretched his neck and started to sniff her hand.

She gave a soft gasp as the horse's nose touched her skin. "I can't believe I'm doing this."

"I can. You're doing just fine." Kirk noticed that Josh was staring at the horse.

Sabre gave a gentle snort and Vanessa laughed. "His breath is so warm," she whispered in amazement.

"See, I told you he likes you. Now pat his nose. He likes that, too."

"I—"

Out of the blue, Josh gave a small chortle and startled them.

Vanessa quickly dropped her hand and stepped back, the moment over. "That's enough for now."

Kirk smoothed his hand down Sabre's neck, soothing him in case he was unsettled, but to his credit the old guy didn't look fazed. "I think Josh likes you, too," he teased the horse. Then he turned to Vanessa. He was proud of her. "You did good, lady."

Her green eyes still held a sparkle of excitement. "Yeah, I did, didn't I?"

The blood rushed to his head. God, she was so beautiful. He wanted to kiss her. She was just too darn tempting with that gorgeous mouth made to be beneath a man's lips.

The air suddenly suspended.

As if she knew this could lead somewhere, she began to look flustered. "Um…I should go back to the house." She edged away. "I have to prepare lunch and change Josh's diaper and—" She twirled around. "I'll see you back there," she called over her shoulder, and hurried back along the dirt path, carrying her son in her arms.

Kirk let her go. If he called her back—Josh or no Josh—he would kiss her.

Six

Vanessa tensed when Kirk came in for lunch not long after she returned from the paddock, but she needn't have worried that anything had changed between them. He was business as usual, his face back to being remote. And for that she was thankful. She was having a hard enough time coming to terms with wanting Kirk so soon after her husband's death. She dared not risk letting these feelings of attraction for Kirk go any further.

The rest of the day was uneventful. Josh took a longer nap than usual in the afternoon. It had been a big day for him, what with all the fussing by his grandparents, then going to see the horses. She let him stay up and eat dinner with them, but he'd been mischievously naughty all through it, not that she minded. She was glad her little boy had a playful streak in him.

However, she *did* mind when she'd put him down in his

crib for the second time and he started to cry again. He'd been perfectly fine when she'd picked him up and taken him out to the kitchen and he had wanted to play.

"Okay, young man," Vanessa said firmly. "Sleep."

His crying became louder.

"No, I'm not going to pick you up again." She tucked him in with the sheet, gave him his teddy bear and left the room, determined to let him cry himself to sleep. Sometimes that was all a parent could do.

Ten minutes later she was in the kitchen finishing the cleaning up and he was still crying. She'd peeped a look into his room once and seen he was okay, but now the sound was getting to her. He was tired and upset and she was getting tired and upset, too.

"Is he okay?" Kirk said from behind her in the doorway.

She swung around from wiping the sink down. "Yes, he'll be all right in a minute."

"He's been crying for some time now."

She bit her lip. "I'm sorry if he's bothering you." She quickly dropped the cloth. "I'll go and—"

"He's not bothering me. I'm concerned that he's in pain."

His concern warmed her. "I looked in on him a short while ago and he was okay. He's got a clean diaper and he's not hungry. He's just overtired." She wiped her hands on a towel then headed for the door where Kirk was standing. "But I'll go see to him."

"Bring him into the living room and we'll watch some television."

"Oh, but—"

"It might help him to settle."

"I have a television in my room. We can watch it in there like I always do."

His forehead creased as she came up close, but instead of

stepping back and letting her pass he curled his fingers around her arm, stopping her. "Is that why you stay in your room each night? You think I don't want you using the television in the living room?"

She'd thought it safer to stay in her own room. That way she'd be in no danger of anything happening between them. "I'm perfectly happy with that. As I'm sure Martha was happy with that arrangement, too," she said pointedly, ignoring the way his touch affected her.

Josh cried again and Kirk's mouth clamped in a thin line but he didn't say a word. He turned and walked away with firm purpose.

"Kirk, where are you going?" she said in spite of knowing. No answer.

"Kirk, honestly, you don't have to do this." She hurried up behind him. "I can take care of my son."

"I know, but he's crying so there's obviously a problem."

"Look, I can handle this." She waited for him to stop but he didn't. "I'm sure you have to get back to your bookwork."

"I don't." He pushed open the bedroom door. "Hey now, what's all this noise about?" he said, his voice softening as he spoke to her son.

Josh was so surprised that his mouth froze mid-cry.

Kirk walked straight over to him and picked him up out of his crib before her son could react. "What's the problem, sport?"

Vanessa could only stand there for a few seconds and stare at Kirk like Josh was doing. Until this afternoon she hadn't thought Kirk was the type of man totally at ease with a small child, but he'd been so careful with Josh around the horse, and now this....

She found her voice. "Kirk, he's had a busy day and now he's out of routine, that's all it is. It'll take him a while to settle down tonight. Just leave him and I'll look after him." She'd rock her son in her arms all night if need be to keep him quiet.

Kirk carried Josh toward her. "A bit of television will help settle him then," he said, clearly used to being in command. "Bring his teddy bear. And that small toy car." He walked past her with her son in his arms. "Make some coffee, too, will you?"

Her mind went blank. "Coffee?"

He stopped. "Hot and strong." His expression shifted, his blue eyes darkened. "I've got a feeling I'll be tossing and turning tonight anyway."

With that comment everything came back to *them*.

Like it had this afternoon.

He headed toward the living room and she was grateful he didn't see her reddening cheeks. Ever since standing too close to him at the horse paddock, the intense physical awareness had flared between them again, leaving her feeling exposed and vulnerable. And at dinner tonight she hadn't needed to see the banked heat in his eyes to know he'd wanted to throw her over his shoulder and carry her off to his bedroom. The worst thing was that she would probably have let him.

Dear God, how did he do it? How did he fuel this ache inside her? More important, how was she going to get through the next part of the evening when every pore of her skin, every breath in her body, craved Kirk's touch? Maybe she should simply let him make love to her.

Simply?

There was nothing simple about any of this.

She took a deep breath on her way to the kitchen and tried to put it into perspective. Kirk was good at making her feel all soft inside, but she could imagine he'd make any woman feel that way. He was an attractive man. Any woman would want him, let alone *her*—a woman whose sex life had been almost nonexistent even before her husband died.

On top of all that, those past few months before Mike's death she'd been so tired from giving birth and looking after a newborn baby, she hadn't given her husband much attention. And Mike had been so caught up in his work he hadn't had time for her, either. They'd lived together and they'd slept together but their lovemaking had been sporadic at best.

So didn't it make sense that abstinence was making her feel everything with an intensity she had never experienced before? Didn't it make sense that her body was coming to life?

But not her heart.

No, not that, she told herself, as her mind shuddered to a screeching halt. She'd been through too much pain losing Mike, she couldn't face getting emotionally involved right now. She had to focus on other things.

Like spending time with her son.

Like making coffee for her employer.

Her *all-too-sexy* employer.

She blinked as the description eased something inside her and made everything less tense. Wasn't she making more of this than she should? Wasn't this all about the obvious, not what was in the shadows? Physical attraction, that was all it was.

Feeling better, she shook off her emotions and reached for the coffee jar. Coffee was what she needed to make right now, not mountains out of molehills.

Coffee for her *all-too-sexy* boss.

All at once her gaze slid to the jar beside the one she normally used. Martha's notes had said Kirk was very particular about his coffee. She smiled to herself.

A short while later she placed Kirk's mug of coffee on the table beside him.

"Thanks." Carefully he adjusted Josh on his lap, then held

the mug to the other side where he could take a sip without spilling it on her son.

She waited.

"Decaf!"

So, Martha had been right.

"Is it?" Her eyes widened innocently. "I find it hard to tell the difference."

She expected him to smile, only he didn't. He stared at her with eyes that missed nothing. Somehow he knew she'd done it to deflect the tension between them.

And then a corner of his mouth crooked with wryness. "Read the label next time, sweetheart. It'll give you a clue."

Sweetheart?

It didn't mean a thing.

"Would you like me to make you another one?"

"It's probably best you don't."

She sank into the armchair and sipped at her coffee, frustrated that he'd seen right through her joke. She'd hoped her little prank would dim the undercurrents between them. It hadn't. The awareness was still there, more so because Kirk knew what she'd been about. She didn't like him being one step ahead of her.

Josh made a noise right then and her gaze fell to her son, glad he looked happy enough on Kirk's lap. She turned to watch the television, but soon found herself drawn back to the other pair as Kirk spoke to Josh about the toy car. She became conscious that it wasn't merely Kirk's focus on her son she found fascinating. It was the interaction between the two. Josh was thoroughly mesmerized, and Kirk appeared equally engrossed in the small boy.

Unexpected tears pricked at her eyes. Now *this* was how she imagined a father to be. How she would like to think *Mike* would have been with his son.

So why hadn't it been?

She blinked rapidly, shocked at her thoughts. Why was she thinking such a disloyal thing? Mike had loved Josh.

He should have found time for his son.

Oh, God, it was true. She was kidding herself to believe it had all been wine and roses. Mike had been so busy solving the problems of the world, he hadn't always had time to be there for her or Josh. Even when Josh was born, Mike had been a bit too irritable with his son, especially if things had been stressful with his police work. And nothing had changed until Mike's death six months later.

She'd understood.

And yet she hadn't.

At all times her son came first for her.

So why hadn't it been the same for Mike?

Kirk looked up at her and his eyes sharpened. "You okay?"

She took a ragged breath and jumped to her feet, not wanting to think about all this. "I'll just go wash these mugs," she said, hurrying away, feeling his eyes following her every step.

Once in the kitchen, she told herself that instead of criticizing her late husband she should remember that Mike had wanted to make a difference. He *had* made a difference. She was proud of him and she'd make sure that her son was proud of his daddy, too. One day when Josh was old enough to understand, she'd tell him all about his father and the difference his too-short life had made to others.

With the kitchen in a sparkling condition again, she went back to the living room and found the television off and her son asleep on Kirk's lap. "Thank goodness," she said softly, half afraid to talk loudly in case she woke him.

"He's out for the count," Kirk murmured, an odd tenderness in his eyes before he carefully heaved himself up out of the chair, her son still in his arms.

She led the way to the bedroom, where he placed Josh in his crib and she covered him with a light blanket and they left the room.

She peeked up at Kirk as she gently closed the door behind them, suddenly aware the two of them were standing close together. "He shouldn't wake up now," she whispered, for something to say.

"No, he shouldn't." He kept his voice low.

A moment inched by.

She cleared her throat. "Um...thank you for your help."

"You're welcome." His voice dropped a notch.

She looked down the hallway, wanting to hurry off to her room. A room that was only a few yards away from where she was now standing.

Kirk was closer.

She looked up at him, ready to say good-night.

Ready for flight.

"Tell me," he said, his words stopping her from moving. "Why did you look like you were going to cry before?"

"Wh-when?" she stammered, but she knew.

"You were looking at me and Josh like you were going to burst into tears." His piercing eyes contrasted with his relaxed stance. "Was it because of your husband?"

Her throat clogged up. "Yes."

"I'm not trying to replace him, you know. With Josh, that is."

"I know. I—" She reached out and placed her hand on his forearm.

They both stilled.

Were both surprised by the touch.

They stared at each other. Then their bodies swayed closer. Their heads inched together.

And finally...finally and a day...their lips met.

She opened her mouth and sighed into him. He groaned, or maybe it was she who moaned. She wasn't sure who made the sound. It didn't matter. Nothing mattered except the feel of his tongue tasting hers, gliding over hers in long, slow strokes that had her swallowing his very breath, wanting all of him.

Every breath he took.

He drew back and she became aware of being lifted against him and carried. Of a handle being turned. A door opened then closed again, shutting them in. Then he let her body slide slowly down him until her feet touched the ground.

She saw they were in her bedroom, yet she was more conscious of being pressed against Kirk's lean length. The soft glow of moonlight filtered through the curtains, yet she was intensely aware of how it reflected on the contours of his face. She inhaled the night air wafting in through the open window, but only Kirk's scent made her skin shiver with delight.

"You are *so* beautiful," he murmured, his eyes caressing her face, making her heartbeat stagger, sending a ripple of anticipation through her.

She knew what was about to happen, and knew she couldn't stop it.

Wouldn't stop it.

Not now.

She needed this.

Needed *him*.

His lips descended and began trailing kisses down the sensitive skin of her neck, his touch making her feel more and more boneless, as if she would sink to the floor any second.

Then he kissed her again, running the tip of his tongue around her lips. He did it one more time, then dipped his tongue inside her mouth, kissing her until she was dizzy with wanting him.

A long moment later he ended the kiss and leaned back a little. Both of them drew breath.

Their eyes locked as he began to undo her top button. Then he undid the next one. And the next. Her blouse fell open, revealing white lacy cups beneath the crest of her breasts. The darkening desire in his eyes made her senses spin as he slipped the blouse off her shoulders, taking care with her injured shoulder. Her bra went next.

In the blink of an eye he slid his palms up and over her ribs until her breasts weighed in his hands. She quivered as he savored them, gently squeezing her nipples until she groaned and leaned her head forward against his chest while he played a game of slow hands.

Exquisitely slow.

Deliciously slow.

Wonderfully slow.

Don't stop.

When he did, she gave a little whimper.

But his fingers soon worked the zipper of her jeans and pulled downward. Denim swept over her hips, her thighs, her legs, as if he was peeling a peach. Her panties followed. She stepped out of them.

He kissed his way up her flank as he straightened. Their mouths met and their tongues began to play while his hands gripped her hips, arching her hard against him, his trousers delightfully rough against her bare skin.

Her senses flooded as his hands slid from her hips to her bottom and he fondled her from behind. In the front, her tautened nipples pressed his muscled chest, trying to find relief but merely craving more.

And then he eased back and bent his head to her breast, taking her nipple in his mouth and sucking. He held her other breast to ransom until she begged him to kiss her there as well. He did, but it was a dip in the ocean to what was swelling inside her. She wanted him naked, too.

Boldly, she broke off the kiss and placed little kisses along his jaw, then down his neck to his chest. She reached for his shirt and fumbled with undoing it before somehow sliding it off his broad shoulders. Next, her hands went to his belt buckle, then his trousers and she stripped him. There was an urgency here. She needed this man. Needed him inside her.

"Vanessa," he muttered.

And then the world slowed.

Her gaze lowered to his hard, gloriously male body standing there, wanting to reach out and touch what would soon be part of her, but not quite bold enough now. His gaze connected with hers and his eyes darkened. Swallowing hard, he lifted her hand and placed it on his erection.

She stilled in shock, then appreciated how wondrous this moment was between them. For the first time ever she held this man in the palm of her hand.

Her fingers began to move, exploring the shape of him, the length of him. He was so hard. In the moonlight she could even see a little vein throbbing along the column of his shaft.

"No more," he rasped, shuddering. He gripped her hand beneath his, stopping her.

Then he led her to the bed, easing her down on it. He lowered himself next to her and began to touch her with a special type of sweetness that echoed deep inside her heart. Before too long she was completely ready to know this man intimately.

With a look that said he understood, he took a condom from his wallet and sheathed himself. Then he nuzzled the entrance at the top of her thighs with his erection. The length of him slowly entered her, filled her, making her complete.

She closed around him, the moment so awesome she cried out his name. He smothered her mouth with a hungry kiss and began to move inside her.

Deeper.

Faster.

Harder.

She had nowhere to go but up…up in flames.

She took him with her.

Kirk kissed Vanessa one last time, then rolled off the bed and went into the bathroom. He'd promised he wouldn't touch her but that promise was now broken. He'd wanted her, he'd touched her, he'd taken her. He hadn't been able to stop himself. Not when she'd wanted him, too.

God, what was wrong with him? He usually had more willpower than this. Now he was involved in a way he didn't want to be, with a woman who'd been through so much in her life. A woman who seemed so much more than the other women he'd bedded.

Yet was she?

Hell, this wasn't a fling he knew would only last a few weeks. She was going to be around here—living with him—for the next six months, and the thought of any emotional entanglements on her part scared the bejeezus out of him.

It was too late now—for both of them. Vanessa had known what she was doing. They were adults. She was responsible for her actions, like he was his own. This was the start of an affair that they'd both entered with eyes wide open. He'd just have to take special care with this woman and make sure he didn't let her manipulate him.

And that was easier said than done when he came out of the bathroom and saw her face down on the pillows quietly crying.

He sat down on the edge of the bed and put his hand on her back. "Vanessa?"

She gasped and spun around. "Kirk?" She hiccupped. "I thought you'd gone."

He ignored a strange tug inside him.

"Is that why you're crying?" he asked, handing her some tissues from the bedside table.

She shook her head.

He scowled. "Then what's the matter?"

She hiccupped again. "I'd only ever been…" sob "…with my husband."

He felt like someone punched him in the gut. She was feeling guilty for making love to *him* instead of her husband. It was obviously far too soon for her to get involved with any man. He should have known this would happen, dammit.

Sliding onto the bed, he leaned back against the headboard and gathered her against him. "Come here," he said gruffly.

With a little sob she fit in against his chest and cried some more. He held her until the crying stopped and she had fallen asleep.

And then he slipped out of bed and went back to his own room. Guilt would accompany him from now on. Guilt and anger. Guilt for taking from her what she couldn't afford to give. Anger for forgetting she should never have been here in the first place.

Seven

Sunlight filtered through her eyelids and woke Vanessa the next morning, but that was nothing compared to the dash of reality on opening her eyes and seeing the empty space next to her. She moaned and rolled onto her back to stare at the ceiling. It hurt to look at the crumpled sheets where Kirk had lain beside her…where he'd been a devastation to her senses…where he'd held her while she'd cried.

Last night had been wonderful. She'd never known sex could be like that. But this time she'd actually done more than *feel* as if she'd been unfaithful and betrayed her husband.

Now she'd actually betrayed him.

She knew it was silly to feel guilty. She wasn't really married any longer. Mike wasn't coming back and she was entitled to make a new life for herself.

And yet…she *did* feel guilty. She couldn't shake it. Time had passed and Mike had been dead seven months now. Could she have loved him like she thought she did, seeing she'd fallen so quickly into the arms of another man?

Yes! She had to believe that. Otherwise their marriage—Mike's *life*—would seem like it had never been. She couldn't have that.

As for Kirk, they had to talk. This was all too overwhelming for her. There were too many feelings here, too much happening too soon. She'd ached to be in his arms, yet making love had made matters worse for her. She hadn't planned on getting involved like this.

Thankfully she heard Josh awake in his room. Her throat constricted as she went in and picked him up. This little guy was her everything. If it hadn't been for him, she wasn't sure she could have gone on living. Josh had been the *only* reason she had gotten up each morning. The *only* reason she'd put one foot in front of the other and picked up the threads of her life.

It was for Josh she would try to put her guilt aside. And it was for Josh she needed to stay away from any further complications with Kirk.

Feeling better after her self-talk, she showered and dressed, then carried Josh to the kitchen. Her breath caught when she saw Kirk finishing up his breakfast. She'd thought he'd already left the house. Now she had to quickly compose herself.

And that was so difficult when she could see a very masculine glint at the back of his eyes. She swallowed nervously. "Er...good morning," she said, breaking eye contact to slip Josh into his high chair.

"Good morning."

She buckled the straps, then looked up to see Kirk watching her. Her stomach began to churn. She had to do this. She couldn't let him think they had anything going here.

"Kirk, about last night...."

Almost at once there was a stillness about him. Then a look of withdrawal came over his face. "You don't have to worry on that score, Vanessa. I don't plan on sharing your bed again."

"You don't?" she blurted out, then blushed. Had he found her boring? Inadequate in some way? Had her tears afterward been too much for him?

All of the above?

She forced herself to look him in the eye. "May I ask why not?"

"You're not ready for a new relationship."

Her heart rose inside her chest. None of the above. He was thinking of *her*.

She tried to appear nonchalant. "Well, I guess there's nothing more to say then."

"No. Not a thing." A muscle began to tick in his jaw. "I suggest we get on with our work." He pushed himself up from the table. "I'll be in my study doing bookwork this morning." He strode past her.

Vanessa stood there, listening to his footsteps fade until Josh required her attention. She had hoped Kirk would go out this morning. She needed this time away from his presence to help straighten out her tumbling thoughts, especially after what he'd just said. She hadn't expected he wouldn't want to continue a physical relationship with her. It went to show that the man was an enigma.

And all that was pushed to the back of her mind when a sedan drew up in the driveway midmorning. Her stomach dropped in dismay. She thought it was her in-laws again.

It was much, much worse.

"Hello there. I'm Pauline Morris," the young woman said in a friendly manner as Vanessa pushed opened the screen door. "And you're Vanessa Hamilton, I presume?"

Vanessa adjusted Josh on her hip. "Yes, I am."

"And this little one is Joshua?"

Vanessa frowned. "Yes, but how do you know what?"

"I'm a welfare worker." She handed Vanessa a government identification card. "I see you're new to the area and I wanted to stop by and see you."

"Oh, my God," Vanessa whispered, looking at the card that indeed proved who she was. This wasn't a chance visit. Not at all.

"There's nothing to be concerned about. I'm simply here for a little chat."

Vanessa felt numb all over. She felt sure that Grace and Rupert had sent a welfare worker to check on her. They'd only been here yesterday. They must have pulled out all the stops for this.

"Perhaps we could go inside?" Pauline suggested, looking more like someone who should be still in a classroom than not.

She pulled herself together and nodded, then led the way inside to the formal living room and gestured to sit down. She was having trouble finding her voice. What in God's name had Grace and Rupert gone and done?

"I'd love a cold drink," the other woman said. "It's a long drive out here."

"Of course, I'm so sorry." She'd been so unbalanced by the welfare worker's sudden arrival that she'd forgotten her manners.

"Here. Put Joshua on the sofa next to me. He can keep me company until you get back."

Vanessa hesitated. She didn't want to leave her son with just anyone.

"He'll be all right," Pauline assured her, a light in her eyes that she said may be young but she was no fool.

Okay, so if the woman wasn't a fool then that could go in *her* favor, she decided, putting Josh down beside Pauline then hurrying into the kitchen, still not wanting to leave Josh alone with the woman for too long.

Her hands were shaking so much she spilled the soda over the side of the glass. As she reached for the paper towel, she saw the light flashing on the telephone extension in the study. Oh, heavens. She'd forgotten Kirk was still in the house. He'd been on the telephone on and off all morning, but if he came out, what would he think with more visitors here because of her? She swallowed hard. Did she really care what he thought right now? Her son was being evaluated by a government official.

And so was *she*.

And she needed to instill herself with confidence, she told herself, as she took a deep breath. She couldn't let her fears get to her in front of this woman. She had to sound normal and responsible and show that she was a loving parent to her son.

Somehow she managed to smile as she went back into the living room. "I hope he hasn't been too much trouble," she said, hoping to sound composed.

"Not at all. He's a good little boy, aren't you, Joshua?"

Vanessa passed the welfare worker the glass of the ice-cold liquid. "I'll go get his playpen so that I can put him down on the floor to play."

"Does he use his playpen a lot?" Pauline asked, almost too casually.

Vanessa hid her agitation at the question. "No, only when I can't keep an eye on him while I'm working."

Pauline took a sip of her drink, then, "So you leave him in the playpen alone while you work in the rest of the house?"

"No. I take him with me." She tried to disguise her annoyance. "As I said, if need be, I'll take the playpen along as well."

"I see."

Vanessa wasn't sure what the welfare worker saw but she didn't like it. She very much feared that her young age and possible inexperience may well bring a reliance on textbooks and not observation.

She quickly got his playpen from the room next door and had it up in next to no time, then put Josh inside. He immediately crawled to get to some toys in the other corner.

"He's not walking yet?" Pauline asked, no criticism in her voice but Vanessa knew her son's development was being recorded.

"No, but he's a fast crawler," she pointed out, taking a seat opposite.

"No doubt he'll be walking soon."

"Perhaps. A lot of children don't stick to a timetable with these sort of things, as you would know. They develop at their pace."

"That's true." Pauline put her glass on the table, then leaned back on the sofa. "Now, I believe your husband died six months ago, so I'd like to offer my deepest sympathy."

"It's seven months ago now, but thank you." It was possible someone else had told her about Mike but Vanessa knew it had come from Grace. She'd bet her life on it.

"And how are you coping with everything?"

Vanessa couldn't stop her chin from lifting. "I'm doing just fine and so is my son."

"That's what I'm here to find out. Joshua's had so much upheaval already in his young life. I merely want to make sure that he's coping with it all as well."

Vanessa could feel herself getting upset. "Look at him. He's a happy and well-adjusted child and he's growing normally and eating well and just because he's not walking yet…" Emotion choked her throat. "I love him so much."

Pauline's eyes softened. "Vanessa, I don't doubt your love for him. That's easy to see." There was a slight pause. "But sometimes things aren't so clear with children. One so young can't tell us how they feel about things."

She swallowed hard before she could speak. "If I thought my son needed some sort of help, I would get it for him."

"I'm glad to hear that."

Vanessa suddenly had to know. "It was my parents-in-law who contacted you, wasn't it?"

Pauline's face remained blank. "I really couldn't say."

"Look, the reason I'm here is *because* of my parents-in-law. They want to take Josh from me and raise him as their own. That's what this is all about. It's not about my son being underdeveloped or at risk or any other thing they can drum up."

Pauline considered her. "Sometimes accepting a little help is not such a bad thing."

Vanessa realized the woman wasn't listening to what she was saying. "Believe me, it would be this time. You don't know these people. You don't—"

"What's going on here?"

Vanessa looked up to see Kirk standing in the doorway with a deep scowl on his face, and all at once she knew that it didn't look good to this welfare worker that she lived here with a single man, even as his housekeeper. She could deny it all she liked, but Grace and Rupert would certainly have made her sound an unfit mother, as though she was jumping into bed with any man, putting herself first and her son second.

And whether that was something a welfare worker could use against her, she didn't know. What she *did* know was that it gave the wrong impression. And if there was even the slightest chance of Pauline ticking the wrong box in regards to Josh, then *she* had to do something right now about it.

There was only one thing that came to mind.

"Darling," she said, jumping to her feet and rushing toward Kirk, her eyes desperately warning him to keep quiet. "This is Pauline Morris. She's a welfare worker. She's come to check on Josh."

"Has she?" he said ominously, having instantly realized who was behind all this, for which Vanessa was grateful.

"Darling, I know how you feel and I've been getting a bit upset about it myself," she said, slipping her arm through his and feeling his muscles tighten. "But it's not Pauline's fault that she doesn't know the full story about Josh's grandparents."

"No, it isn't," he agreed, but there was a question in his eyes for *her* alone. He wanted to know what *she* was doing. Right now.

She turned back to the other woman. "Kirk has asked me to marry him and I've said yes," she lied, feeling him stiffen beside her in shock. She smiled up at him. "Darling, I'm sorry. I know we decided not to tell anyone just yet but it's *important* she knows." She smiled back at Pauline. "We're engaged but we're keeping it between ourselves for the moment. We didn't tell Grace and Rupert for fear of upsetting them."

Pauline blinked. "Oh…I see."

"I loved my late husband, Pauline, and I'm sure he would have approved." She paused, unable to say she was in love with Kirk. "The Deverills have lived here many years and have an excellent reputation," she said, remembering Linda telling her that. "Kirk will be a wonderful husband and father."

"I'm new to the area, so I'm afraid I don't know everyone

here yet." Pauline eyed Kirk, then her eyelashes fluttered the tiniest bit. "But I'm sure Mr. Deverill would be wonderful."

Vanessa was shocked. The woman was *flirting* with him?

Before she could think what to say next, Kirk gave the woman a warm smile. "I'm sure you'll still make your assessment on how you find Josh, not because Vanessa and I are getting married," he said, a hint of steel behind his words.

Pauline immediately lost her coquettishness. "Of course. It's the only way to do things."

"Good." Kirk led Vanessa back to one of the chairs and sat her down before he scooped up Josh from the playpen. The small boy curled into him as if they were father and son, and Vanessa's heart squeezed for a second as Kirk sat in the other chair with Josh on his lap.

He smiled again at the welfare worker. "Fire away with any questions. I'm happy to help in any way I can."

"That's very nice of you, Mr. Deverill," Pauline said primly, as if to make up for her earlier transgression.

"Well, it's important that your mind is at ease about us." He smiled down at Josh, who reached forward and tried to pull at his hair. Kirk chuckled and Josh giggled back, trying to repeat the action. "As you can see, he's a healthy, happy little boy and I love him like a son already."

The breath left Vanessa's body at the words. She knew Kirk was only saying that for the other woman's benefit, but he was very convincing. For a split second she wished he *did* love her son and that they really *were* engaged to be married.

Then sanity returned.

Pauline looked satisfied. "Yes, I can see that he adores you." She turned away to take a notebook out of her handbag. "I just have a couple more questions then I'll be on my way."

Fifteen minutes later, the woman put the notebook away. "Thank you both for your assistance."

Vanessa went to speak, but it was Kirk who got the question out first. "What happens now?"

"Nothing. I can see no justification for the complaint."

"Thank God!" Vanessa said, feeling almost faint with relief as she looked across at Kirk and her son and blinked back tears.

Then she remembered Grace and Rupert. "Do you report back to…the people who complained?"

"No. I work for the government, not the complainant. If anyone asks they will get a standard response with no details." She hesitated. "Of course, they're free to make another complaint if they feel it's warranted."

"This complaint wasn't warranted in the first place," Kirk pointed out, his face taut with anger.

"I know but we have to check these things out."

Vanessa bit her lip. "So you won't mention my…our…engagement to them?"

"It's not up to me." Pauline stood up. "Though I do think it's best sometimes to bring things out in the open with some people, don't you? That way they can't accuse you of keeping them out of the child's life."

Vanessa stood up, too, as well as Kirk. "I suppose so," she agreed, but she knew it wasn't the case with her in-laws.

"Think about it."

"I will." She'd think of nothing else.

They saw the woman off from the verandah, then Vanessa slumped down on one of the wicker chairs, her legs finally going out from under her. She'd got through this but it wasn't over yet. Not with Grace and Rupert. Not by a long shot.

Then she looked up and saw Kirk's hostile glare.

And she knew it wasn't over with him, either.

It was just the beginning.

She hopped up from the chair. "Here. Give me Josh. He

needs to take a nap." She didn't look at Kirk as she took her son out of his arms.

"Come and see me when you've finished," he ground out, as if he could barely talk.

Oh, Lord.

She got Josh settled and was soon stepping back on the verandah, though not soon enough by the look on Kirk's face.

She held up her hand. "I know what you're going to say."

"That's good, because words fail me." His angry gaze held hers. "Actually no, they don't. You're unbelievable. Why you said what you did is beyond me."

She drew herself up. "Grace and Rupert want to take my son away from me. They'll stop at nothing, or hadn't you noticed? They're after my son."

"I noticed, but you didn't have to say we were engaged, for Christ's sake."

She shifted uneasily. "I know. I didn't think. It's just that Pauline had been grilling me about Josh and frightening me and it wasn't looking too good, and then you came in and it seemed like the best idea at the time."

"If that's the best, I'd hate to see your worst."

"Look, I thought it might help convince Pauline that Josh had a stable family life." She angled her chin. "I'll do what's necessary to keep my son."

Something altered in his expression. "And if they put in another complaint in six months' time and we're not married, what then? By then you'll have gone from here and the welfare worker will think you're either a liar or unstable. It'll be documented that you go from one man to another, move from place to place. The only thing you've helped along will be your in-laws' conviction that Josh needs saving. From you."

She leaned against the verandah post. "Oh, God. I never thought of that."

"Didn't you?"

Her eyes widened. "What do you mean?"

"Marriage is what you were aiming for, wasn't it?"

She quickly shook her head. "No! I didn't. I—"

"Enough lying. You're trying to get someone to marry you and you'll use any means—any *person*—to keep your son." His lips twisted. "I guess I'm just damn lucky I was the one on hand," he snapped, seeming to look even angrier.

"No! I have no intention of marrying you—or anyone else for that matter. I've lost my husband only recently, for God's sake," she said, her voice catching.

"That didn't stop you sleeping with me last night, did it?"

She sucked in a breath. "That was a mistake. We've already agreed not to repeat it."

"I told you before I don't like being used."

"I'm sorry. If I could take it back without harming my son then I would." She hesitated. "Let's just keep this to ourselves and no one else. Pauline believes we're engaged and she's the only one. I'll worry how that will look once I leave here."

A nerve pulsed near his temple. "Fine, I'll be your fiancé for now. But I can tell you this, Vanessa. I will *never* be your husband."

He strode inside.

Life settled into a pattern over the next few days as the temperature climbed into the high nineties. Vanessa felt bad for what she'd done to Kirk and she understood why he was upset, but he had to understand that she'd had no choice. Her son was her life. She'd do anything to stop him being taken off her, including using Kirk like that.

She just wished he didn't think she was after marriage. It was the one thing she absolutely did not want—with any man.

And of course, she knew Grace and Rupert wouldn't let things be, but she had no idea what they would do next. She couldn't relax. She could only take comfort in knowing that if push came to shove she had the Deverill name on her side now. Kirk would help her protect her son—even if he didn't like the way it was being done on her part.

One morning Linda called to see how things were going and Vanessa almost burst into tears when she heard her cousin's voice. Until that moment she hadn't felt sorry for herself about the welfare worker's visit, but as soon as Linda started speaking, her feelings very nearly got the better of her. Linda was family. And as a mother she would understand the fear of having her child taken off her.

"Vanessa? Are you there?"

Vanessa cleared her throat. She couldn't tell Linda any of what happened. Her cousin would fret. "Yes, I'm here."

"There's something wrong. What's the matter?"

She took a steadying breath. "I miss you, that's all, you silly goose."

Linda tutted. "You're lonely, aren't you? I should've realized it was too much for a city girl to live on a remote cattle station like that. I'm sorry, Vanessa. I—"

"Linda, I'm not lonely," she cut across her. "I love it here."

She recognized that was the truth. There may not be an ocean on her doorstep, nor soft sand underfoot as waves crashed on the beach beneath a blue sky. But something out here in the outback—something about this untamed country-side—soothed the rawness inside her. There was nothing as bright as an outback sky, nor as light as the wind that rustled the land to life. And nothing like the distinctive smell of eucalyptus, grasses and tree bark all mingling in the air—a smell as unique as the sound of a cackling kookaburra.

"Are you sure?" Linda's voice drew her back to the conversation. "You can tell me the truth. You know I won't hold it against you. Or even Kirk for that matter."

"Linda, I'm fine. Really. It was just hearing your voice. I miss you and Hugh, that's all."

"We miss you, too, sweetie, but I'm so glad it's working out. How's Josh?"

"Fantastic," she said, injecting some enthusiasm in her voice. He was doing just fine.

"How are you getting on with Kirk?"

"He's a very good boss."

But a reluctant fiancé, she mused, then scolded herself. It wasn't a laughing matter.

"I knew he would be. He's sexy, too, huh?" Linda teased.

"Things are working out very well, I'm pleased to say," Vanessa said, ignoring the comment, then heard a noise and saw Kirk in the doorway.

His mouth tightened before he kept on walking. He'd obviously heard what she said and taken it the wrong way. She sighed. What else was new?

After that they spoke some more then Linda ended the call. Vanessa blinked back tears then threw herself into the housework. At dinner that evening, she passed on Linda's regards and gave him an update.

"They're leaving in two weeks' time and asked if we'd go into town to say goodbye. They've got so much going on that it'll be impossible for them to leave Jackaroo Plains to come out here."

He inclined his head. "I'll be there."

"So will Josh and I," she said, ignoring that he was trying to make a point of dividing them. They both knew he'd be taking her and Josh with him. She didn't have a car, for one thing.

He paused between bites of food. "By the way, this weekend I have to go to The Alice for a charity dinner."

She blinked. "Alice Springs?" The town was in the middle of Australia and often referred to as "The Alice" or "Alice" and would take hours to fly there. She didn't want to admit it but she knew she would miss him in spite of his coolness toward her.

"I want you to come along with me."

The suggestion threw her. "Me?" She didn't even have to think about it. "No, thanks."

His mouth twisted. "As my fiancée, I'd think—"

"Very funny."

His expression cleared. "You and Josh are coming to Alice Springs with me and that's that."

Her brows arched. "Josh is invited, too?"

"Of course. Do you think he wouldn't be?" His intense gaze never wavered from her face. "I won't leave you both here while I'm away."

She felt a strange tug inside her chest. "We'll be okay."

"Not if your in-laws find you alone, you won't be."

Warmth spread through her at his concern. He may not like her being in his life, but he was at least adult enough to put that to the side for the sake of a child.

She found herself actually considering it. "I'd like to see Alice Springs," she said cautiously.

"Good. Then it's settled. The dinner's a formal affair and—"

"Wait a minute! I thought I was being asked along for the ride. You didn't mention I had to go to the dinner with you, as well."

"You've got to eat."

She shook her head. "No, I'm sorry. I can't attend the dinner as your partner. Everyone will think we're an item."

His mouth tightened. "I know but that can't be helped."

"But what if someone knows me through Grace and Rupert? What if they tell them I'm there with you?"

"It'll be highly unlikely anyone will recognize you and even if they do, you're still coming with me. It's the lesser of two evils right now."

She couldn't fault his thinking. "Who'll look after Josh while we're at the dinner?"

"The hotel has a very good babysitter who is also a registered nurse. You just need to sign a medical consent form in case Josh needs a doctor when we're not there."

"You've already checked into this?" Why wasn't she surprised?

"Only to allay any of your concerns about leaving Josh with a stranger."

Pleasure softened her heart once more, then she hurriedly subdued it. "Surely you've got someone else to take to this dinner instead of me?"

"I did, but not anymore."

Oh. She was his second choice. That made her feel so good. Not!

"And just to put your mind at rest," he continued, "I've booked their best suite which has a couple of bedrooms. It'll be no different than living here."

Okay....

"By the way, don't worry about an evening dress. I'm happy to buy you one once we get there." She immediately opened her mouth but he got in before her. "I'm sure you hadn't expected to be attending such a formal function during your sojourn in the outback."

He had her there. She'd brought a couple of dresses with

her, just in case, but they were nothing fancy enough for a charity dinner. She wanted to rebel against taking anything more from her employer than necessary, but she couldn't afford to spend money on a suitable dress.

"Thank you."

Of course he probably didn't want to be embarrassed by her off-the-rack clothes, she told herself, then knew that wasn't fair. If he was ashamed to be seen with her, he wouldn't have invited her to the dinner in the first place. He could have simply taken her to Alice Springs and attended the dinner himself.

"We leave midmorning on Saturday then," he said, taking her comment as acceptance.

She left it at that. She was a little excited about the trip, but there was also a ripple of apprehension rolling down her spine. She was sure Kirk didn't have anything untoward planned for them in Alice Springs.

It was what *wasn't* planned that worried her.

Eight

Kirk could have piloted them himself in his own plane but he'd decided instead to hire a plane from Dubbo Airport. He loved flying, but a four-hour flight before attending a high-profile function that evening wasn't something he was keen on doing. Not when he was unsure how Josh would go on the flight and whether Vanessa would need a hand with her son.

An hour into the flight and so far any trepidation had been unfounded. The little boy happily played with his toys on the seat next to his mother, who was looking fantastic in a cream pantsuit that composed her figure into a very classy package. He wasn't a man easily impressed but with this woman he was.

She noticed him watching them. "He'll fall asleep soon," she assured him.

"He's a good kid."

Motherly pride filled her green eyes. "Yes, he is."

Kirk felt his heart catch on something that couldn't be, so he willed himself to return to the paperwork in front of him.

He was aware of Vanessa talking to her son, getting him settled for a nap. Eventually he became absorbed in the report that required his attention far more than this woman opposite.

He wasn't sure how long before he looked up, but when he did, Josh was asleep and Vanessa was sitting there with her eyes closed, breathing softly, taking a nap. He couldn't help himself. For the longest time he sat and stared at her, wanting to reach out and trace her features with his fingertips.

With his lips.

And dammit-all-to-hell he couldn't.

Those lips of hers were treacherous. Too treacherous for a man to forget that he'd heard her gloating to Linda the other day about how well things were working out for her. No bloody wonder she was happy with herself. She'd worked everyone to get what she wanted. He'd never seen a more professional hit. ASIO could do with her in their ranks. As a matter of fact, the staff at the Australian Security Intelligence Organization could easily take on the likes of some of the women he'd known. All of them mistresses of disguises. All disguising what their true intentions had been.

The only good thing to come of this now was that Vanessa was here with him and not Samantha. Months ago when he'd received the invitation, he'd planned on Samantha partnering him this weekend. It burned him up to think how she might still have been pulling the wool over his eyes. And how he probably wouldn't have seen her true colors until after their marriage. He'd had one bloody-lucky escape.

And no woman was going to trap him again, he decided, certainly not the one sitting opposite him right now. Okay, so perhaps he should have left her at home. He could have got one of the wives to stay with her overnight. He hadn't thought of it at the time and that was just as well. The Hamiltons would steamroller over any chaperone.

Anyone except him.

At least this way he could protect her from them.

But he wouldn't marry her.

When Vanessa woke up, he was fully focused on his report again. And at the hotel they were soon settled into their suite. He'd ordered a playpen for Josh so he wouldn't crawl into mischief if their backs were turned, and he'd arranged for one of the top boutiques in the hotel to bring up a selection of dresses for Vanessa for tonight.

And then they were standing there looking at each other across the width of the hotel suite, and he was tempted to walk over to her and pull her into his arms.

Instead, he headed for the door. "I've got to see a man about a bull," he rasped, and left the suite.

It was true he had some business to attend to with a breeder from the Northern Territory, but he knew he'd have gone and sat in the bar if necessary. Being around Vanessa made the blood constantly surge through him like a hot tide, almost devouring him with the pleasure of it. She was killing him with.... Damn, whatever she was doing wasn't deliberate, but she was still killing him.

A couple of hours later he returned to the suite to find Vanessa stretched out on the carpet, stacking toy blocks with Josh and laughing at her son when he knocked them over. For a moment Kirk had an image that this was how it should have been if he'd had a son. How it would have been if he could have given Vanessa a child. If only things had been different.

She looked up then and caught him staring and he pulled himself together. He'd merely been taken unawares.

"Did you find a dress you liked?"

She started getting to her feet. "Yes. It was hard to choose. They were all so beautiful. Thank you."

Like you, he added.

"You should have kept the lot." He went to reach for the telephone. "I'll get them sent up here."

"No, wait! Kirk, it's a lovely thought but I have no need for so many dresses."

She was the housekeeper, nothing more, he reminded himself. "We should take Josh for a swim in the pool," he suggested, then knew he was only taunting himself. Seeing Vanessa in that one-piece she'd worn back at Linda and Hugh's motel wouldn't do his heart rate any good.

As if she knew, a hint of pink stole into her cheeks. "Um…not right now. He's overdue for a nap."

"Maybe later," he said, watching her pick Josh up off the floor and flee to the bedroom.

In the end, Josh slept longer than expected and they didn't even get to the pool. It didn't matter. Kirk's heart rate still managed to go sky-high when Vanessa came out of the bedroom dressed in a slinky emerald-green evening gown that sparkled as she glided toward him.

She twirled around. "Is this okay?"

His heart thumped wildly as his eyes drank her in. From the top of her stylish blond chignon to those strappy high heels, she looked beautiful and elegant.

"Exquisite," he said thickly.

She gave a small "oh, my," a flush appearing on her high cheekbones. The doorbell went and she spun away. "Er…that must be the babysitter," she said, her voice sounding a little breathy as she hurried to answer it.

He became conscious that his own breathing was a little unsteady and he knew that she wasn't the one killing him. *He* was the one cutting his own throat.

By the time introductions were made with the babysitter, his breathing was back under control. He eyed the young woman, who was around twenty-five and appeared to be capable and friendly, then Vanessa left her cell phone number with the woman and they left the suite.

"Josh seemed to take to her," Vanessa said, her manner composed on the ride down the elevator to the ballroom.

"The hotel assures me she's the best at what she does. Her references were glowing."

"That's good to know."

"Yes." He knew what she meant. He'd never leave a child with anyone he didn't trust.

The elevator stopped and he cupped her elbow to escort her into the ballroom. As he turned to give his tickets to the person at the door, he caught her sneak a look at him in his dinner suit. It had only been a glimpse but it was enough to get his pulse racing again.

"You didn't tell me we were at the top table," she whispered as he walked her up the center of the room. He could feel eyes upon them but he didn't care. People would gossip.

"Just relax and enjoy yourself."

"Around you?" she said with a dash of unexpected humor.

"I'm not so bad."

"You're not so good, either."

He gave a low chuckle. "See. You're enjoying yourself already."

She smiled. "True."

His gaze zeroed in on that smile but he was forced to drag his eyes away as they reached their table. He wished them anywhere but here. He wanted to keep on looking at a certain delectable mouth and—

"Kirk!"

He felt himself go rigid when he saw the woman sitting at the table. "Hello, Samantha."

She jumped to her feet and kissed him full on the mouth,

then pulled back and looked down at her husband. "Darling, look who's here. It's Kirk."

"Yes, I see." Her husband gave a smirk that set Kirk's teeth on edge. "Hello, Kirk."

"Roger," he acknowledged, with a brief handshake. The older man seemed to think he'd won some sort of top prize in his wife. If he only knew....

"Oh, it's so good to see you," Samantha enthused. "Come and sit next to me right here, darling."

Kirk held back. "Don't you want to be introduced to my date?" he mocked, and cupped Vanessa's elbow again, bringing her in closer. "Vanessa, this is Roger Marks and his wife, Samantha." He deliberately introduced Roger first.

Vanessa smiled at them but he could feel the tenseness in her body. She would be astute enough to know something was going on here.

Samantha's smile stayed in place but her eyes narrowed. "I didn't know you were seeing anyone, darling."

"Didn't you?" he said smoothly, and left it at that.

Unfortunately he had no choice but to sit next to Samantha. It was either that or put Vanessa between them and he couldn't do that to her. He wasn't quite that cruel. So he was stuck between the two women. It was going to be a tough evening, he decided, watching as the other guests began introducing themselves. Most of them were business acquaintances.

After that, food and speeches were served over the next hour. Samantha continually tried to steal his attention but he ignored her. Still, for all his worldly experience he found it disgusting when she whispered that she'd love to meet him for a private drink somewhere after the dinner. Clearly she was hinting at an affair.

Vanessa was in complete contrast. At first she stayed quiet, and he saw her open her evening purse and glance at her cell a couple of times, no doubt checking that all was okay with Josh. Then she started to relax and warm to the other guests and they warmed to her. It wasn't only her beauty but her natural charm that drew them like a magnet and sealed her appeal with them.

If they only knew she was his housekeeper.

Mouth tightening, he pushed back his chair and stood up. "Let's dance." He saw her startled look as he helped her out of her chair.

On the dance floor she went into his arms but stared at him with a furrowed brow. "You're not enjoying yourself?"

"Yes."

They danced a few steps.

"Samantha's beautiful."

"I don't want to talk about her."

"Why not?"

"If I tell you then I'll be talking about her, won't I?" he drawled.

A rueful smile tipped the corners of her mouth, then she looked past him at the other people on the floor. "You know, I really do feel like Cinders at the ball tonight."

His jaw clenched. "Don't say that. You run rings around everyone here. You're too good for most of them and—"

"Kirk?"

He pulled himself up short.

"You think I'm too good for them?"

He realized that was the truth. "Yes."

Her eyes softened. "Thank you for the compliment."

Alarm bells went off in his head. Suddenly he wasn't sure how but his attitude had definitely softened toward her. He suspected it was seeing the two women together that had done it. Samantha just didn't measure up against the woman he knew Vanessa to be. Samantha was a bitch. Vanessa was a sexy witch. Samantha gloried in using people. Vanessa only used people to protect her son. There was a difference that up until now he couldn't accept.

Now he did.

"Did you ever go to these type of functions with your in-laws?" he asked, trying to focus on something other than the moment, then saw her eyes cloud over and realized it was insensitive of him to mention them.

"Not often. Mike and I didn't like the company Grace and Rupert kept."

"I see." He could imagine her in-laws' friends. He knew the type. Many of the same sort were here tonight. How could the Hamiltons not appreciate this woman? She had grace and class and was an excellent mother. Then his thoughts paused. Perhaps they *had* seen it and been more than a little jealous of the woman who'd stolen their son? And now their grandson.

Vanessa deserved better.

The music ended with a crash of cymbals that startled them both, and they smiled at each other before returning to their table, where Vanessa picked up her purse and headed to the ladies' room. Kirk watched her leave. Samantha tried to get his attention but he ignored her. The room seemed rather flat now.

Ten minutes later he saw Vanessa coming across the room. God, she was so beautiful. And then she smiled at him as she came closer and that socked the air right out of him. He could do nothing but watch her gliding toward him. Nothing but—

Just then, an older lady awkwardly got to her feet in front of Vanessa, took a step and slipped. Vanessa reached out for her but the other woman grabbed hold of both Vanessa and the tablecloth, taking them down with the plates and glasses.

In an instant Kirk was on his feet. By the time he'd rushed over, Vanessa was crouched down helping the woman and others were gathering. Vanessa appeared to be uninjured, thank God, but the older woman was catching her breath. Kirk recognized her immediately.

"Are you okay?" Vanessa was saying as she moved aside a piece of broken plate near the woman's head.

The lady winced. "I think I'm just bruised." She tried to sit up.

"Don't move." Vanessa looked around her. "Is there a doctor here?"

A man was pushing through the crowd. "I'm her grandson." He fell to his knees. "Grandma, I'm here. Are you okay? I—"

Suddenly another man pushed through the crowd. "I'm a doctor. Now let's see…"

Vanessa went to get to her feet but the woman caught her hand. "Your dress. It's ruined."

Vanessa didn't even look down at herself. "Forget about it, love. The main thing is that you're okay."

"You're so sweet…"

Kirk helped Vanessa to her feet and handed her the purse she dropped, and they both stood watching as the doctor checked the woman over. An ambulance was called as a precautionary measure.

"Come on." Kirk began leading her from the room. "There's nothing more we can do here." Out of the corner of his eye he saw Samantha flirting with another woman's husband and he was appalled by her lack of integrity.

"Do you really think she's okay?" Vanessa said, cutting across his thoughts.

"She'll be fine." He continued out the door.

At the elevator she glanced down at herself and grimaced.

"I'm a mess. I should have let you buy me another dress in case of something like this. I—"

"I've had enough tonight. We won't be returning to the dinner."

She blinked. "But it's only nine-thirty and you came all this way and—"

"I've put in an appearance. That's all that matters." He punched the button for the elevator. "Do you know who that woman was?"

She shook her head, her forehead creasing. "No."

"Lady Mabel Standish."

Her eyes widened. "The ex-Prime Minister's mother? I didn't realize."

"I know you didn't."

Her face filled with dismay. "Oh, my God, I'm sorry. I've embarrassed you by calling her 'love' and not by her title."

He swore. "You didn't embarrass me at all. I'm impressed by your caring for a stranger, if anything."

"You are?" She blinked. "Well, thank you."

The elevator doors slid open and several other people joined them. Two elderly women exclaimed over the stains on Vanessa's dress and their conversation took up most of the ride.

Kirk watched Vanessa charm the other ladies with her good humor and he knew Samantha wouldn't be taking it in stride like Vanessa had. In the first place, Samantha would never have helped another person. And right now Samantha would be ignoring these ladies in her hurry to get to her room for a change of clothes so that she could get back to the action.

Vanessa stepped out of the elevator and hurried forward, eager to get to her room now and change out of her dress. Her hands were sticky from the chocolate dessert that had spilled all down the front of her.

As soon as Kirk opened the door to the suite, Rhonda jumped up from the sofa and stalked toward them. Her gaze went over Vanessa's dress before snapping back up to her face disapprovingly. "Your son has been sick."

Vanessa felt herself pale. "Wh-what?"

Rhonda seemed to take pity on her. "He's sleeping peacefully now but he vomited a couple of times."

Vanessa was already on her way to the bedroom as guilt swamped her. She'd been downstairs enjoying herself while Josh had been up here being sick. "Did you call a doctor?"

"Yes. He's the hotel doctor and he said it was just a stomach upset. But it was as well you signed that medical consent form. I couldn't get in touch with you."

"Why didn't you call me on my cell phone?"

"I did."

"What!" Vanessa stopped in her tracks and took her cell phone out of her purse. She groaned. "Oh, no. There's two unanswered calls." She glanced up at Rhonda. "I didn't see them. I had my phone on silent so it wouldn't ring during the speeches."

"Perhaps you should have checked more often then," Rhonda said, making her feel even guiltier.

"You could have sent a message," she heard Kirk say tersely behind her.

"I did. Twice."

Vanessa looked at Kirk. "We didn't get any message, did we?"

"No."

The woman drew herself up straighter. "Well, I definitely sent one. The front desk assured me they would pass it on."

"They didn't," Kirk told the babysitter.

Rhonda looked doubtful, but Vanessa didn't bother arguing. The main thing was that she was here now.

She spun on her heel and continued to the bedroom where her sleeping son lay. She sagged against the crib when she saw he really was sleeping. "His cheeks are a bit red but he looks okay, thank God."

"The doctor gave him some medicine to bring his temperature down."

Vanessa reached down to softly touch his hair but then pulled back. She didn't want to wake him.

She looked at the babysitter. "Thank you for looking after my little boy so well, Rhonda. You did the right thing in calling the doctor."

Rhonda's face relaxed. "He's a lovely little chap. I'm sorry he was sick." She waited a moment. "Now that you're back I'll be leaving."

"I'll see you out," Kirk said, and walked her to the door.

A few moments later Vanessa heard him behind her in the doorway. "Do you think it was the flight here?" she asked, turning to look at him.

Kirk's brows knitted together. "I'm not sure."

"What if he gets sick on the flight back?"

"That's not until Sunday. We'll get the doctor to give him the okay first. If he's not ready to travel, we'll wait until he is."

A lump welled in her throat. She and Josh could find their own way back once he was well if necessary, but Kirk's consideration touched her deeply.

"Why don't you go change your dress?" Kirk said, easing off his tie. "I'll make us a drink. I think we could each do with one."

Vanessa nodded and grabbed some casual slacks and a knit top to change into in the bathroom. She didn't bother with shoes. If she'd been alone she would have pulled on the bathrobe supplied by the hotel, but she wouldn't feel comfortable having a drink with Kirk half-dressed.

She'd just walked into the bedroom to check on Josh when the smell of vomit hit her.

"He's been a little sick again," Kirk said, doing his best to move Josh away from the mess.

She grabbed some tissues and helped clean Josh up as best she could. His forehead was hot to the touch. "I'll take him in the bathroom and sponge him down."

"I'll call the doctor while you do that."

"Thanks." Her stomach churned with anxiety.

The doctor was still in the hotel and arrived as Vanessa carried Josh back into the bedroom around fifteen minutes later. She thought it might be the doctor who'd helped Lady Standish, but this man wasn't dressed in a dinner suit like the other doctor had been.

As he checked over Josh, Vanessa was vaguely aware that Kirk had stripped the crib down and remade it with a sheet from her bed. He'd opened the balcony door, too. Night air ruffled the curtains and freshened the room.

Ten minutes later the doctor left again, after giving Josh a thorough going over and declaring him fine. "I don't think you'll have any more problems with him tonight. He's over the worst."

Thank God!

Kirk saw the doctor out while Vanessa drew the clean sheet over her son and got him settled. By the time Kirk came back, his little eyelashes were lowered in sleep.

"He'll be fine now," he said quietly from the doorway.

It was reassuring having Kirk here with her and helping her like this. It made her feel less alone. A feeling she could easily get used to with this man. If she let herself.

Her mind spun away from that thought. "You didn't have to clean up in here, you know."

"You were busy with Josh."

"I could have managed, but thanks anyway. I appreciate it."

"You're welcome."

Suddenly the moment was bonded by a sense of family. The thought frightened her. "I'd better go take a shower then get some sleep," she said, her pulse skipping a beat when she saw his eyes flicker. "Good night, Kirk."

There was enough of a pause to make an impact.

"Good night, Vanessa." He pulled the door closed behind him.

In the shower, she couldn't shake off the notion that she and Josh had bonded with Kirk tonight in a way she hadn't expected. And that was all the more strange because they *weren't* a family and it was silly to even think it. She simply appreciated Kirk's help tonight, that was all. Certainly Mike would never have helped out like that.

She finished her shower and wrapped herself in the thick hotel bathrobe; then realizing she was quite thirsty, she opened the bedroom door to get a bottle of mineral water from the bar.

She got a shock when she saw Kirk sitting back on the sofa in the lamplight, his tie long gone, his jacket off. He held a glass of whiskey in his hand. She'd expected he'd have gone to bed by now.

He leaned forward. "Is Josh okay?"

"He's still sleeping," she said, putting his mind at rest. "I'm thirsty so I thought I'd get a bottle of mineral water."

Ice clinked in his glass as he pointed it at the bar. "Help yourself."

"Thanks."

"Join me for a while."

His words stilled her. "Um…okay."

It only took a few seconds to get her drink, then she took a seat on the opposite sofa, pretending to concentrate on un-screwing the small bottle, but aware of everything about him.

She looked up as she took a sip and her eyes focused on Kirk. Whether it was the growing lateness of the hour, or the shadows dancing on the wall, the intimacy of the room reminded her of making love with him. Had she really been in his arms? It still seemed unbelievable he knew her body so intimately. That she knew his.

"Thanks again for helping me tonight," she said, somehow keeping her voice steady.

"It was nothing."

"No, it was really nice of you. Mike would never have cleaned up vomit like you did." She made sure she didn't sound critical of her late husband, but Kirk deserved to know that what he'd done was something noteworthy.

He paused. "Tell me about him."

"Mi-Mike?"

He considered her. "What was he like?"

She wasn't sure why he was asking, but it surprised her to know she didn't mind talking about Mike tonight. Oddly enough it didn't hurt as much anymore. Right now she didn't feel guilty about wanting to talk to another man about her late husband.

"Well, he was a good man, Kirk. I could tell that right from the start. Handsome, too. My friends were interested in him but he said he only had eyes for me."

"I can understand why."

She gave a gentle smile of thanks, then focused on trying to remember what now seemed so long ago. "He loved being a policeman. It was important to him. It was who he was. He liked helping people and fixing the wrongs of the world." Her heart filled with wry tenderness. "I think he thought I needed him."

"And did you?"

If she were to be honest…

"Not at first, but after a while I fell in love with him. Then after my mother remarried and went to live in England, it was kind of nice to have someone of my own."

For too short a time.

She took a shuddering breath. "He didn't deserve to die. He was only stopping in at the bank so that he could sort out a problem with our account." No need to mention his spending had created the problem in the first place. "Grace and Rupert had offered to loan us some money to help buy a new car, you see, but Mike wouldn't take it." She had to give him credit for that. He had never, ever taken money from his parents.

"I used to think if only he hadn't gone into that bank, if only one of the customers hadn't become hysterical, then Mike wouldn't have tried to help her and gotten shot because of it. Then I realized that him being the kind of guy he was, it wouldn't have mattered. Somewhere, sometime, someone else would have needed his help," she said, her throat clogging up. "He just couldn't stop being a hero."

A moment ticked by.

"He sounds great," Kirk said thickly.

Her heart squeezed tight. "He was but—"

"But?"

She chewed her lip, not sure why she'd said that but the look on Kirk's face said he wouldn't let it go. "Mike's job kept him really busy," she said, trying not to sound unsympathetic. "So it wasn't always possible to put us first."

"Then he was a fool."

"Wh-what?" No one had ever said anything like that before.

"The guy had a gorgeous wife and a beautiful baby son and he preferred his work over you both?" Kirk fixed her with a candid gaze. "Yes, he was a fool."

Vanessa should have been offended but she actually felt a

sense of release as something expanded inside her. It was a relief to know that someone else could see what she'd only recently recognized about Mike.

"*I* wouldn't make that mistake," Kirk said quietly.

She looked at him and knew he spoke the truth. "Why have you never married, Kirk?"

His mouth set in a grim line and she thought he wasn't going to answer. Then, "I was going to ask someone, but she married another man."

She sensed who that was. "Samantha?"

He nodded. "I started going out with her about six months ago in Sydney. We seemed compatible so I decided it was time I got married. I was about to ask her to be my wife when she up and married Roger."

It didn't sound very romantic, but with some men, who could tell what they felt?

"Did you… Do you love her?"

A swift shadow of anger swept across his face. "No. She only used me to get to someone like Roger, though I have no doubt she would have married me if he hadn't come along. I had a lucky escape."

"I'm sorry."

"Don't be."

He must have been shocked to see Samantha here tonight. "You might find someone else eventually."

"I'm not looking."

"But there'd be plenty of women who—"

"I'm sterile, Vanessa."

She stared.

Just stared.

Then, "Dear God," she whispered.

He held her gaze, a tick beating in his cheekbone, and she could only stare back, stunned.

Then he put his glass on the coffee table and got up from the sofa to go stand at the window, looking out into the darkness beyond. There was a terrible tenseness to his broad shoulders.

Finally he turned. "I found out during a paternity test when I was at university in Sydney," he said, his voice devoid of any emotion. "We had used protection, so I suspected Jillian was lying. She did it to protect her married lover."

He'd never have children.

She fumbled to find the words. "I'm so sorry, Kirk."

He acknowledged her comment with a nod of his head. "And then there was Samantha. She was the kind of woman who didn't want children. I thought we could have a good life together. Thank God I hadn't told her about my sterility."

Samantha's desertion must have been another blow to him, especially after that first woman had lied to him. She couldn't imagine he'd allow himself to get hurt again after either of those things. He was a proud man after all.

"Not many people know about my sterility," he continued. "Just my family. And Jillian, of course, but she disappeared from my life long ago."

Her heart rolled over. "Then I'm honored you told me," she said huskily, conscious of how much it must have cost this proud man to tell her something so very personal and private.

Dear heaven, how dreadful for him never to father a child.

Never to hold his baby in his arms.

Never to leave something of himself behind.

At least *she* had the experience of being a parent. Nothing could take that away from her.

She hurt for him.

All at once she knew what she had to do. She wanted to touch him, become a part of him, share his pain. He may not have wanted her in his home, but he had taken her in anyway and had been there for her against Grace and Rupert. She'd be there for him this time.

She eased herself off the sofa and walked over to him, feeling him go rigid when she slipped her arms around his waist and pressed her cheek against his chest. Time capsuled around the two of them as she let herself listen to his thudding heartbeat through the soft material of his shirt.

"Vanessa?" he muttered, his hands finally coming up to grip her shoulders.

She inched back and looked up at him, letting him see not pity, but her need to comfort him. "Kirk, I want you."

His eyes blazed, then banked. "No." He went to push her away.

She held strong against him. "And you want me," she murmured.

He stiffened further. "I don't... I can't."

"You do." She noted he wasn't pushing her away any longer. "And yes, you can."

Without giving him any further time to resist her, she went up on her toes and placed her lips against his throat.

"Don't," he growled, but she could hear the weakening in his voice.

It thrilled her.

With growing confidence, she leaned back and helped herself to the buttons on his dress shirt. He was so gorgeous as is, it was a shame to undo them, but those ridged stomach muscles begged to be touched as she pushed his shirt back off his shoulders. Then she tunneled her fingers into the whorls of dark chest hair like they belonged there.

"Stop," he muttered, his eyes fixed on her.

She flexed her fingers, loving the feel of his springy hair. "No," she whispered breathlessly, trying to remember this was for him, not so much for her.

"Stop."

She flexed her fingers again. "Give in, Kirk. Let me have my way."

"No."

A part of her smiled at his stubbornness but the rest of her was far more serious. This was about showing this man he would always be enough for a woman.

She had to.

For his sake.

Ever so slowly she let her fingers drift down over his rib cage, down over his hard stomach, down to the zip of his pants where he felt even harder. She unzipped his trousers and slipped her hand around his erection, loving the guttural sound he made.

She caressed him and heard his throat emit a rich humming that spurred her on. She leaned close to place her lips against his chest, his stomach…then she kissed her way lower and took him in her mouth.

"Vanessa," he rasped, but he threaded his fingers through her hair and held her to him, telling her he wanted this as much as she did. Her heart began skipping beats as she let the tip of her tongue glide over him, tasting him, teasing him, loving the feel of him starting to lose control.

About five seconds later, he growled, "Not here," and lifted her away from him. In one rapid movement he'd drawn his zipper halfway up, then swooped her in his arms. He carried her to his bedroom and laid her down on the bed.

Her stomach fluttered as he pulled back and stood over her, looking so tall, so male, so incredibly honed in his half-done-up trousers and a bare chest begging to be stroked.

"Condom," he said, about to turn away.

Quickly she collected her thoughts. "No, Kirk."

His head went back in shock. "No?"

"I want to feel *all* of you inside me," she said huskily. "I don't want anything between us."

His eyes glinted with an inner light. "Are you sure?"

"Absolutely."

A moment passed…followed by another.

All at once he knelt down beside the bed and thanked her with a long, deep kiss. Then he took control of her body with his lips and his hands, until her head was spinning and her heart was pounding, until he brought her to an overwhelming climax before joining with her, and she was left wondering exactly *who* was the most giving tonight.

As the last tremors subsided, Kirk drank in the sight of the woman beneath him. He'd never seen a more gorgeous woman, with her golden mist of hair, her peach-tinted skin, her overwhelming beauty. It felt so good to be inside her like this…feeling her around him… He'd never made love to a woman with no barriers between them before.

No barriers in more ways than one.

God, he couldn't believe he'd actually told her about his sterility. Did she know there was something special going on here? She had to know this was more than sex.

But how much more?

For both their sakes, he dared not find out.

Nine

A child's giggle pulled Vanessa out of a deep slumber the next morning and she opened her eyes to find Kirk crouched down beside the bed with Josh in his arms.

"I think your son wants his breakfast."

It took her a moment to waken fully.

"Josh!" She flew into a sitting position. "He's okay now?" she asked, noting his cheeks were no longer red. "Yes, he seems okay," she answered herself. She'd checked on him a couple of times in the night as well.

Then she'd come back to bed.

And into Kirk's arms.

All at once she saw the flare in Kirk's eyes as he looked down at her naked breasts. She flushed and pulled the sheet up to cover herself.

"It's a bit late for that," he muttered, putting Josh on the bed beside her. "I have to go out for a couple of hours. Just ring downstairs for anything you need." He started walking toward the door. "If Josh is okay later, we'll go down to the pool."

"That would be—" He was gone before the last word was out of her mouth. "Nice."

She was disappointed they wouldn't be sharing breakfast together, but more disappointed that he seemed withdrawn from her again. After last night she thought he might…that they might…what? Nothing. She hadn't really thought anything. There was nothing *to* think about. They'd made love, that was all. She'd given everything of herself but had asked for nothing back. Just because he *had* given back didn't mean a thing.

He returned to their suite late morning, and took her totally by surprise with a kiss that felt as if he'd been waiting hours to do that very thing, but as if by unspoken agreement, neither of them mentioned this latest development between them. It was too new for her. And she was sure Kirk didn't want to get involved any more than he was.

They spent an hour in the shaded area beside the hotel pool. Kirk's gaze had drifted over her floral-green one-piece with appreciation, and she hadn't been able to ignore her pounding heart at seeing him in board shorts. It made him look younger and more carefree.

So she was rather glad that Josh was full of energy and wanting her attention. He loved the water, having fully recovered from his upset tummy last night. She watched as Kirk walked around the shallow end of the pool with Josh on his shoulders, and her heart brimmed over with love for her son.

Then she looked at Kirk. What a wonderful father he would have made, so patient and kind, like he was with Josh. She could even picture Kirk's children with his dark hair and blue eyes, their pudgy little arms wrapped around his neck, his house filled with laughter and love. The thought that it would never happen for him brought a lump to her throat and she quickly got out of the pool and went to sit at the table.

They were eating a light lunch a short time later when out of the corner of her eye Vanessa saw Samantha bearing down on them in a bikini that was almost indecent. Kirk would have to be made of stone not to want this woman, at least physically.

An unusual feeling curled in the pit of her stomach at the thought of Kirk and Samantha together. For a moment she didn't recognize it but then realized it was jealousy. Her heart tilted at the admission. She'd never been jealous of Mike, so why was she jealous now?

"There you are, darling," Samantha said, sashaying more as she got closer. "I've been looking all over for you. I thought we were going to catch up on old times."

Vanessa stiffened and sneaked a look at Kirk. Had he gone out to meet his ex-lover this morning? He hadn't said it was a business engagement.

His face hardened. "There's nothing to catch up on," he said, and something inside Vanessa slipped back into place. He was telling the truth. He *was* made of stone where Samantha was concerned.

"Don't be like that, darling." Samantha pouted, then her gaze slid across to Vanessa and Josh. "Oh, you're a mother, too."

"Yes, I am," Vanessa said, proud of that fact.

Samantha looked at Kirk. "I didn't know you were the type to play daddy, darling."

"And I didn't know you knew what type I was." In a dismissive gesture, he turned away and handed Josh a slice of a peach. "Don't let us keep you."

Samantha's lips tightened a fraction before she stretched her lips in a feline manner. "I must go find my husband. I promised I'd give him a long, slow massage," she said suggestively, before sashaying away.

They both watched her depart.

"Roger shouldn't turn his back on that woman," Kirk muttered.

"Yeah, he's likely to find a knife in it."

He chuckled and she smiled back and all at once any tension between them slid away like melted butter on a summer's day.

After that Josh started to cry from tiredness, and they went back to their suite. At no time did Vanessa feel that Kirk wanted to push Josh aside to get to her.

But once Josh was asleep, Kirk pulled her into his arms and made love to her, then they fell asleep, too, only waking up when someone rang the doorbell to the suite and delivered a package. It was a new dress, compliments of Lady Mabel Standish.

Vanessa wore it to a private dinner between her and Kirk later that evening in their suite, then he stripped it off her and made love to her again.

Afterward he pulled her up against him on the bed and brushed his lips against her hair. "How would you like to go hot-air ballooning with me at dawn tomorrow?"

She tilted her head back. "Are you serious? I'd love it." Then she bit her lip. "But what about Josh?"

"The babysitter will look after him for a couple of hours. It's all arranged."

She offered him a smile, touched by his consideration. "That would be lovely."

"Let's get some sleep," he murmured in her ear.

Vanessa felt his chest beneath her cheek and his arm around her, cradling her close to him. He didn't let her go even after his breathing deepened and he'd fallen into a deep slumber.

It took her longer to get to sleep. She was really happy in what seemed such a long time and she wanted to savor this feeling. Tomorrow would come soon enough. And tomorrow she'd wonder where all this would lead.

⁕

Pre-dawn, Kirk woke her with a languorous kiss then quickly made love to her, before playfully dragging her out of bed in time for the babysitter to arrive. It wasn't Rhonda this time but another woman the hotel had checked out and who seemed perfectly capable of looking after a small child. Thankfully, Josh was still over his upset stomach from the other night, and after peeking in on him, they left the hotel room.

Vanessa was really excited about taking this hot-air balloon ride. It was still dark and her excitement grew as they drove under an outback sky alight with stars, arriving at the launch site to see the balloon being inflated. Kirk had chartered a private flight and soon they were climbing into the basket. Then they began to move, and silently they rose in the air just as the sun illuminated the horizon over the Australian desert.

The exhilaration was unbelievable as they soared high, the immensity and remoteness of the landscape stretching endlessly beneath them. They spotted kangaroos and wallabies amongst the spinifex grasses, trees came alive with budgerigars and cockatoos.

Then they floated toward the ancient MacDonnell Ranges and the impact of it all took her breath away. "It's stunning," she whispered in awe.

Silence, then, "Yes," Kirk murmured beside her. "*She* is."

His tone drew her to look at him and she felt giddy all of a sudden at the intense look in his eyes. He was talking about *her.* Her heart did a double dip.

She cleared her throat, then tried to make light of it all. "Of course you mean 'she' as in Alice Springs, right?"

His lips curved. "You're pretty cheeky for so early in the morning. It must be the outback air."

"Oh, so *that's* where you get it from?"

He gave a low chuckle and she grinned back, then an eagle swooped by, capturing his attention and breaking the moment between them.

And then something happened inside Vanessa as she watched him looking out over the world. *His* world. Out here, the comparison of their lives and their problems in the scheme of things didn't really matter. Everything was down to basics in the outback. Survival of the fittest. A person had to be in tune with nature if they were to survive. Kirk was such a man. He was as in tune with himself as he was with nature.

Her heart turned over.

She loved him.

The realization imploded in her head without warning.

She loved him.

It felt so right. So complete. She couldn't remember the last time she'd felt so warm in her bones. The realness of Kirk in her life touched her deep inside.

And then she froze.

She remembered Mike. She couldn't go through the pain of losing again. She wouldn't survive another loss. A loss that would be a hundred times worse this time because she loved Kirk far more than she ever loved Mike. With all her heart. With all her soul. She'd rather live without him than go through worse heartache again.

All at once she realized he was looking at her.

His brows had drawn together. "What's the matter?"

Her heart stopped for a moment, before she quickly averted her face and gestured toward their surroundings. "It's just so beautiful," she said, not wanting him to see the emotions rioting through her. He was so close to her, inside and out. She dared not let him get even a hint at what was going through her right now.

Unaware of her thoughts, he slipped his arm around her waist and pulled her against him and together they stood looking out over the sweeping vista. She'd never forget this moment with him. It was engraved in her heart.

They left Alice Springs after lunch. Kirk had a briefcase full of papers to work on during the trip and occasionally he'd look up, or Josh would catch his attention, but Vanessa was grateful he didn't want to talk about anything deep and meaningful. Instead she gazed out the airplane window as the miles slipped by, knowing that somehow she had to lock away the knowledge of her newfound love and make sure Kirk never discovered it.

Oh, God, just a few short months ago any thought of involvement with a man had only been a shadow in her mind and a very long way in the future, not this affinity she felt with Kirk so soon after her husband's death. An affinity that overrode the memory of Mike and replaced it with a living, breathing man who made her feel so very much alive again.

Did she make Kirk feel as alive?

The thought caught her off guard. Here she was thinking about herself, but what did he think about her? How did he *feel* about her? And in the long run did it really matter?

No.

She instinctively knew he wasn't prepared to hand her his heart, or even offer her marriage. He'd been about to do that with Samantha when she'd betrayed him. And so had Jillian when she'd accused him of fathering a child that wasn't his. He wouldn't let himself risk being betrayed again. He'd made that quite clear when he'd accused her of engineering their "engagement" for the welfare worker.

And that was just as well. The last thing she wanted to do was repeat history and hurt him when she had to move on at the end of her six months.

They arrived back at Deverill Downs in the early evening and Vanessa's throat tightened as Kirk drove up the winding dirt road toward the house. This was his home. And now it had come to mean so much more to her.

Because of Kirk.

And that begged a question she hadn't let herself ask before. It wouldn't look good for her in front of the welfare worker, but should she leave rather than stay until the six months was up? Surely she could convince Pauline or any other social worker that it was best to realize her mistake now than in six months' time? Wouldn't that make her look mature and caring of her son?

As for leaving Kirk…wouldn't it be best to walk away now…while she still could?

That thought was on her mind as they went inside the house and she put Josh in his playpen while Kirk carried in their things. She was walking past him when he suddenly pulled her up against him and thoroughly kissed her.

Love washed over her.

He eased back. "I want you to move your things into my room."

Her heart wobbled as she looked up at his handsome face. It was tempting, but in that moment she knew the lovely fairy tale had come to an end. "I can't, Kirk. I'm sorry." She swallowed hard and said what she had to say before her courage deserted her. "I think I should leave."

He sucked in a sharp breath. "What's brought this on?"

"It's all getting rather complicated, isn't it?" She couldn't say more or he might probe further.

His eyes closed in on her. "Is this to do with my sterility?"

"God, no." Not directly. And only then because he'd never let himself fall in love with her. She winced inwardly. Not that she wanted him to. Then there *would* be complications.

"Well, then," he said, evidently believing her. "Nothing's really changed."

And that said it all.

She didn't flinch. "You're right. Nothing's changed. You're still my employer and I still work for you."

And she had nothing to fear from him. It may sound cold and callous—and she knew that wasn't the case—but he would only want her for the next five months and that was all.

Fine.

So why not stay and enjoy their time together? He wouldn't stop her from eventually leaving. She knew that. In fact, his wanting her to go would then be the catalyst she could use to help her walk away.

"Okay, I'll stay, but I still won't move into your room."

He blinked almost in slow motion, his eyelids lowering, then lifting. "Why?"

The intense look made her gaze dart away. She needed her own space, that was why. Otherwise it would be doubly hard to leave when the time came.

"It wouldn't feel right." She tried to think of more excuses, anything to back up her decision. "Besides, what if your mother comes home?"

He sent her a dry look. "Perhaps she'll give us a permission note," he mocked, then drew her close and kissed her hard. He pulled back. "Be prepared. You may not share my bed but there's no way I'm not sharing yours." Before she could think, he let her go and turned to walk away. "And if my mother turns up," he drawled, over his shoulder. "Too bloody bad."

Vanessa's heart pounded beneath her breast, pleased despite herself. And wasn't it typical that he hadn't given her a choice? She could only pray the one thing he *did* give her was enough heart space to let her breathe.

No sooner had she finished preparing Josh a drink and had put the coffee on, than she looked up and saw Kirk in the doorway, a piece of paper in his hand. He had a very serious look in his eyes that made her place the two mugs on the bench.

"There was a fax on my machine," he said, a pulse ticking in his cheekbone. "It's for you."

Her eyebrows lifted. "Me?"

"It's from a lawyer's office in Sydney."

"What!" Her heart sank as she raced over and snatched the paper from his hands. She read it and felt the blood leach from her face. "It's from Grace and Rupert. They're taking me to court for custody of Josh."

He nodded. "I read it."

"They say I'm an unfit mother," she whispered, her heart squeezing tight.

"That's bullshit. There's no way they can prove something that isn't true."

"You don't know these people, Kirk."

"I've met them. I know what they are."

She was hardly listening now. "I'll call them!" She twisted and grabbed at her cell phone that was sitting on the bench. She kept it with her at all times so Grace couldn't accuse her of keeping their grandson from… Her hands shook so much she couldn't even see the numbers.

Kirk took the cell from her. "Here, let me get them on the line for you. But first, take some deep breaths. You need to stay calm. That'll knock them right off balance."

He was right.

She took deep breaths and counted to ten, making herself focus on what she would say. She had to think clearly. This was too important to screw up. Then she nodded for him to continue.

"Good girl," he murmured, handing her the phone as soon as he'd dialed.

Grace answered on the first ring. She'd obviously been waiting. For a split second when she heard her mother-in-law's voice Vanessa went blank, then she rallied. She needed to do this right.

"Grace, what's this letter about?" she said, somehow making herself sound firm and cool, not a weepy mess of fear like she was inside.

There was a short silence.

"What it says, Vanessa." Her mother-in-law was equally cool. Unfortunately she didn't sound the least off balance.

Keep going.

"I don't understand, Grace. I'm a good mother. How can you say I'm not?"

"According to the nurse at the hotel in Alice Springs you're not."

Vanessa's stomach sank. "Nurse? You mean the babysitter?"

"Yes. She's a nurse, too, you know. That'll carry a lot of weight in a courtroom. The private investigator we hired was very thorough."

She sucked in a sharp breath. "You hired a private investigator to follow me?"

"Yes. And the nurse signed an affidavit this morning that you were out enjoying yourself with your lover while your son was being sick back in the hotel room. You even returned to the suite with food all over your dress. That must have been some party, Vanessa."

"But we didn't know Josh was sick," Vanessa said, her anxiety growing.

"She said she called you on your cell phone to tell you that Joshua was sick and you wouldn't answer. And she sent messages via the front desk and you ignored them."

"We didn't receive the messages from the front desk, and I'd put my cell phone on silent so that it wouldn't interrupt the proceedings. But I checked it often."

"Not often enough obviously." Grace said, hitting Vanessa right where it hurt.

"You may have convinced that welfare worker that Josh is fine but we know different now, don't we?" Grace paused. "We also have a copy of the hotel records stating that the doctor was called out not once but twice to check on Joshua."

"It was a stomach upset, that's all."

"You might have gotten away with that except you were seen swimming in the pool with your lover and Joshua the next day. I have pictures of Joshua crying and not wanting to be there."

Vanessa was beginning to feel sick herself. "That's not true. He was fine by then and having a great time. He only started crying because he was tired."

"And there's pictures of you and your employer together," Grace continued, almost spitting the words at Vanessa. "You were both out enjoying yourself hot-air ballooning at dawn this morning." She paused for effect. "Where was your son then, my dear?"

The evidence compiled was damning. Her mother-in-law was making it look as though she would be the worst person to bring up a child.

"You can't do this," Vanessa said weakly, all the fight gone out of her now.

"I'm afraid we can. I owe it to my Michael." Grace ended the call.

Vanessa stood and stared at Kirk. It was impossible to

stop the fear in her heart. "She's going to do it," she muttered in disbelief. "She's actually going to take Josh away from me."

His jaw clenched as he took the cell phone from her hand and put it on the bench. "I heard."

It hit her then that her in-laws had the upper hand. They would take Josh away from her. They could even stop her from seeing her son. He would die under their domination.

And she would die without him.

"I have to go to Sydney. I have to speak to her face-to-face." She headed for the door.

Kirk grabbed her arm, bringing her to a stop. "It won't do you any good. The woman is as hard as nails. She'll see that as a weakness and you'll be forever in her clutches."

She knew all that. "Yes, but at least I'll have my son."

"Don't do it, Vanessa."

"I have to."

"Think about it."

She pulled away from him. "Think about what? Think about what I'll do without Josh? What Josh will do under their control? What Josh will do without *me?*" Her voice cracked on the last word.

Kirk's eyes gentled. "Take it easy, sweetheart."

Her pain was too great. Panic erupted inside her. "Easy? That's *easy* for you to say. *You* don't have a son to lose."

His head reeled back.

She bit down on her tongue.

Oh…God. She'd said the unforgivable. To the man she loved.

"Kirk, I'm sorry. I'm—"

"No, you're right," he said stiffly.

"But I didn't mean it like that." How could she have said something so terrible to him?

"I understand, Vanessa." He gave a brief pause. "Just

grant me one favor? Give me twenty-four hours before you do anything."

She scrutinized his face. "Why?"

"I want to speak to Rhonda and see if I can sort things out."

That was so good of him but, "What can you do, Kirk? The way the private investigator presented the evidence was pretty damning." Her heart caught at the injustice of it.

A steely look entered his eyes. "I'll find a way."

She considered what he was asking of her. Her initial reaction was to get on the first plane to Sydney and beg Grace not to proceed with the custody battle. A day may make all the difference.

Then she looked at Kirk. She owed him this. And if he could help...

"Okay."

The tension in his shoulders eased a little. "Right. First thing tomorrow I'm flying myself back to Alice Springs."

"I'll come with you."

"No, you stay here with Josh. He doesn't need another long plane journey right now."

A tinkle of warmth ran through her at his consideration. "But your work? You must have other important things to do."

"Not as important as this." He strode from the room.

Not long after she heard him drive off down the road toward the cattle yards. She instinctively knew that when he returned he *wouldn't* be sharing her bed tonight.

She'd hurt him deeply.

Yet *still* he was prepared to help them.

Here was proof that Kirk wasn't like Mike. Kirk was putting her and Josh before everything else. She drew a painful breath. God, how she loved this wonderful man.

Ten

Kirk decided to hire a pilot to fly him back to Alice Springs. Doing a round-trip in one day was grueling, especially when he had so much to do when he arrived, and he needed all his concentration to work out a plan of attack. He'd do whatever it took to clear Vanessa's name.

It had to be enough.

Dammit, he'd make sure it was.

By the time he arrived at the hotel, at Kirk's request the manager was waiting with Rhonda in the office. Kirk had also arranged for an acquaintance of his to be there, too, wanting an independent witness in case anything went wrong.

He got the preliminaries out of the way first, then he spoke direct to Rhonda. "Let me get this straight. A private detective approached you the morning after the charity dinner with documentation showing you that a welfare worker had been called in recently to check on Joshua Hamilton. Is that right?"

"Yes." Hostility was bouncing off her.

"Did it occur to you that anyone can provide information to a welfare worker and that it could be false?"

"Of course, but coupled with my messages being ignored about the child being sick, I could see that their concerns were valid."

"Really?" Kirk snapped, then turned to the manager. "The child's mother doesn't deny that she turned her cell phone to silent, but that doesn't excuse your front desk staff for not passing on the other messages. What is the procedure for something like this? Who takes responsibility for the messages being passed on from the front desk?"

The hotel manager drew himself up straight. "Mr. Deverill, I can assure you that the reception staff know not to hold on to an important message such as this. They would make sure it reached the parents."

That wasn't good enough.

"In this case they didn't, did they? So obviously something went wrong."

"Mr. Deverill, believe me—"

"Who was on duty at reception on Saturday night?"

"Mr. Deverill, I don't think we need go that far."

Kirk seared him with his eyes. "A loving mother may lose her child over this, Mr. Beecham. I'd say we haven't gone nearly far enough."

Mr. Beecham winced then picked up his phone and gave a few instructions. "They'll let me know shortly," he said, hanging up.

"I want to speak to the doctor as well," Kirk shot at him.

"That may not be so easy. Dr. Potter left for a vacation in Hong Kong only this morning. He'd still be in the air."

"Then get him on his cell phone, Mr. Beecham."

The manager's mouth tightened. "Mr. Deverill, I really must insist that—"

"Mr. Beecham, if this matter isn't sorted out within the next hour I'm going to sue whoever owns this hotel for getting involved in matters that had nothing to do with it." He turned to Rhonda. "And you, Nurse Laker, should be ashamed of yourself."

She bristled with indignation. "I only did what I thought was right."

"The right thing to do was speak to the welfare worker in charge of the case before jumping in feet first. Or better still, pass your concerns on to a welfare worker here in Alice Springs and let them run with it. Joshua's mother has got nothing to hide." His mouth thinned with displeasure. "You were duped, Rhonda."

"You have no proof of that."

"I will." He looked at the manager. "I suggest you put a move on with your staff, Mr. Beecham. And it would be for-tuitous of you to pick up that phone and call Dr. Potter right now so he has the message when he lands."

It was amazing what a bit of impetus could accomplish. By three in the afternoon, Kirk had it all down in writing and was on his way back to the airport in a cab, after thanking his friend for his patience. Once they'd taken off, he'd call the private detective who'd returned to Sydney, then he'd phone Vanessa from the plane and put her mind to rest.

God, she must be crazy with worry. He might never know what it was like to lose a son, but as much as it hurt him to hear those words from her mouth, if it felt a quarter as bad as he was feeling at the thought of her losing Josh, she was one helluva woman. But then, deep down he'd already known that.

Vanessa trusted that Kirk would do all he could, but she couldn't help be on tenterhooks the next day. What if he failed to find Rhonda? Or what if Rhonda wouldn't change her mind? What if the private detective had garnered more damaging evidence? She broke out in a cold sweat just thinking about it.

Of course, Kirk would be a formidable adversary.

And so were her in-laws.

And this was her son's life.

Her life.

Dear Lord, last night of all nights she had wanted Kirk's arms around her in bed, yet she couldn't blame him for staying away. She had been cruel to remind him he'd never know the threat of losing a child, despite being almost out of her mind with fear. Her heart ached for him.

Then her heart jumped in her throat when the telephone rang while she was preparing Josh's dinner. She rushed to pick it up, her eyes on Josh in his playpen, her ears attuned to Kirk's voice.

Instead there was a pause. "Who's speaking please?" a woman's voice came down the line.

"This is Mr. Deverill's housekeeper."

"Oh." There was a short silence. "This is Martha."

Vanessa froze. "Martha?"

"I was Kirk's housekeeper, but if he's got someone else in my place then—"

"Martha, no," Vanessa said quickly, hearing the woman getting upset. "I'm only his temporary housekeeper. Mr. Deverill is definitely keeping your job open for you."

"Are you sure?"

"Of course."

"Oh, that's such a relief. I'm coming home next week, you see. My sister didn't really need me at all. She's much better."

Vanessa's heart sank but she attempted to sound casual about it all. "Mr. Deverill will be pleased to have you back."

"I'll be glad to be back. Can you tell Kirk that I called and will see him next Monday?"

"Certainly."

The woman rang off and Vanessa's legs went from under her and she had to go sit at the table. Her job here was almost over. Was this another sign that she should give in and return with Josh to the Hamilton fold? It was looking more and more as though this would be her next option.

And then Kirk called.

"I have good news, Vanessa," he said over the phone.

Her heart skidded to a stop. "You do?"

"Rhonda's retracted her statement."

"Wh-what?"

"She's willing to testify in court that she was given the wrong impression by the private detective. She thought she was helping to save Josh from an unfit mother. And the private detective caved in when I challenged him. He wasn't willing to risk losing his license, so he's provided a damning statement about your in-laws."

It wasn't sinking in. Dared she believe it? "But what happened to the messages Rhonda sent us at the dinner?"

"They were passed on to one of the waiters, who got caught up in other things and didn't know a sick child was involved. I've also got statements from the hotel staff who saw us with Josh at the pool and they confirmed Josh looked fine. The other babysitter did, too."

"I can't believe it," she whispered, tears blinding her.

"The only thing left to do is wait for a call from the hotel doctor. I need to get a statement from him. He was on a plane to Hong Kong and I've left a message for him to call me back, but I'm certain he will support us.

A wave of apprehension swept through her. "Are you sure he won't be a problem?" she asked, wondering if they were getting their hopes up too soon.

"Not at all, so don't give it a second thought."

"But—"

"Vanessa, with all the evidence I've gathered, I can't see how the doctor can refuse to support us."

"I know but—"

"Vanessa, trust me."

His words stopped her panic. Trust the man who'd helped her so much? "I do," she murmured.

"Good," he said, a pleased note to his voice. "Listen, I probably won't get home until around nine tonight. Will you be okay?"

"I will be now." He must be exhausted.

"Call me on my cell phone if you need me. And, Vanessa, don't call Grace yet with the news. Wait until I get there."

Her heart constricted. "Why? Do you think there's going to be a problem?"

"Not at all, but all the same, she won't take kindly to it. I just want to be there for you."

"Oh." That was thoughtful of him.

"How's Josh?"

She looked across at her son. "He's playing with his toy truck."

"Okay. See you tonight." He ended the call.

Vanessa hung up the phone, her heart aching with love for the man who put himself before others. He might appear hard with certain people until they got past his guard, but she now knew that hardness was actually strength of character.

And then she thought of something else.

She hadn't even thanked him for what he'd done for her today.

When Kirk came up the verandah steps later that evening she could only stare at him, unable to look down at the papers in his hand.

"Go on," he said, holding them out to her. "Read them."

She felt like she was moving in low gear as she reached out and took them from him and began to read under the light.

The words blurred but soon she'd read enough to know what he'd told her earlier was true.

"By the way," he added, "the doctor called me back, too. He's fully supporting us."

She flung her arms around his neck and kissed him. "Thank you, Kirk. Thank you so much."

For a moment he held her tight and returned the kiss, then without warning he put her from him. "You need to call your in-laws."

Her happiness dimmed, not at the mention of Grace and Rupert but because the sudden aloofness in Kirk's eyes was beginning to scare her. "Kirk, I—" She saw him stiffen so she changed tack. "Wouldn't the private detective have told them already?"

"The guy's making himself scarce until tomorrow. Believe me, he isn't anxious to get caught in the crossfire." He took his cell phone out of his pocket. "Want me to call them for you?"

It was nice of him to offer, but she shook her head. "No, I'll do it."

He handed her the cell. "Make the call, Vanessa. Then we'll talk."

Her heart sank, but she drew herself up straighter. First things first, she told herself as she concentrated on punching in the numbers.

Once again Grace answered on the first ring with a coldness that went right through Vanessa. "My dear, all communication between us should be through our solicitors from now on."

Vanessa heard the dismissal in the other woman's voice.

She had to speak now before Grace hung up. "There won't be any need for that."

Grace must have thought she'd smelled victory. "So you're giving us our grandson?"

At that point, Vanessa saw red. Her mother-in-law was speaking like their grandson "belonged" to them. As if she was of no importance as Josh's mother and that he wouldn't miss her in his life. The sheer arrogance of it stunned her. The absolute anguish of what they'd tried to do to her tore her insides open.

"No, Grace. You won't be taking my son from me. You see, I'm holding a signed statement by the nurse stating that your private detective lied to her about me." Vanessa was gratified by the other woman's gasp. "And I've got statements from various hotel staff refuting all those ridiculous claims. And best of all, your private detective was very eager to put the blame on you and Rupert for making him twist the truth."

"I don't believe it."

"You don't? I'll fax them to you right now."

Silence.

"Vanessa, look," Grace began to wheedle. "You know I wouldn't have gone through with this. I was merely trying to get you and Josh to come home."

"Grace, if you or Rupert *ever* contact me or my son again I'll put out an intervention order on you and I'll use these papers to show that *you're* the ones who are unfit. Have a nice day." She ended the call.

Her hands were shaking from sheer relief and she saw Kirk looking at her with admiration.

She gave a weak smile as she handed his phone back. "Maybe one day I'll be generous and let them have supervised visits, but not until they've changed. It's going to be a long time before I'm feeling generous toward them."

"You're being generous just by considering them."

She tilted her head. "You wouldn't be as generous, would you?" He would be as fierce when protecting his own, but there would be no second chances with him.

"No, I wouldn't."

And she'd said the unforgivable to him.

No second chances.

Sudden tension swamped the air.

"Now that's resolved," he began, "you and Josh will be fine." He appeared to withdraw from her. "There's no need for you to stay here any longer."

She gasped. "Are you asking me to leave?"

He gave the slightest of pauses. "No, I'm *telling* you to go. It's time for you to move on."

Her heart took a tumble. "It's because of what I said, isn't it?"

"Don't beat yourself up about it, Vanessa. Our relationship was always going to come to an end anyway. It's just happening sooner rather than later."

She knew all that but saying goodbye didn't seem so easy now.

"You have no need to worry about anything," he continued, sounding more like a robot than a lover. "I've got a real estate friend on the Gold Coast. He's found you a nice house to rent close to Linda and Hugh. I've taken out a five-year lease for you. It's all paid up to help you get on your feet." He paused. "I'll take you back to Linda's tomorrow. They're leaving at the end of the week. You can travel with them. They'll understand."

All at once hurt bounced inside her chest and rose in her throat as anger. Walking away from him was different from being *pushed* away. She was too much trouble, obviously. How convenient that he could make arrangements to get rid of her. Was he going to think of her like he did Samantha? In time would she merely be a faint memory to him?

"I don't need your help," she choked, drawing on her pride.

"Yes, you do."

She raised her chin in the air. "You can keep your lease and your money, Kirk. Josh and I will manage just fine."

"You'd better not think about going to your in-laws," he all but growled.

"No, but even if I was it's none of your business. You've done your good deed for the decade, Kirk. You've saved us from the evil clutches of my in-laws. You can now resume your own life and forget all about us."

"Don't be foolish, Vanessa," he said gruffly, putting his hand on her arm.

She shook him off. "You know the funny thing? Martha called today to tell you she was coming back next week. So you see. You had no need to ask me to leave. I would have just gone."

And that was exactly what she did at that moment. She went inside to her room, leaving him standing there. The most foolish thing she'd done was fall in love with a man who didn't want her any longer.

By the time Vanessa reached her room, her legs barely carried her over to the bed. It was slowly sinking in that she had to leave tomorrow. Kirk wanted her gone. The thought tore at the threads of her heart. She could feel the moisture springing to her eyes.

And then she refused to cry.

What was the matter with her? Why was she making an issue of this? It wasn't like he'd made any promises to love and honor her. Up until a few minutes ago she wouldn't have wanted that anyway.

So what had changed?

She had.

Suddenly she knew she couldn't walk away from him. All her reasons for not letting herself fully love Kirk were gone. Now she knew she'd rather live with the fear of losing him, than not have him in her life at all.

She jumped to her feet. She had to tell him she was ready for commitment. Perhaps somehow he would let her stay in his life. He didn't have to love her in return. She had enough for the two of them.

He was standing at his desk in the study, his back to her, going through some papers. Her heart was in her mouth as she stepped inside the room.

She moistened her dry lips. "Kirk, I want to stay."

He spun around and for a moment happiness leaped in his eyes.

Then his face closed up. "Impossible."

"Listen to me. I *need* to stay."

He straightened. "There's no future for us, Vanessa."

"But—"

His mouth flattened in a grim line. "This isn't about me. It's about *you* and what *you* want. What *you* need."

"I need *you*."

"Once you leave here you'll see that you don't."

It struck her then that he wanted her gone because he was protecting her.

From himself.

In spite of being dragged into it, he'd been protecting all along, rescuing her from something or other. She'd hit the nail on the head when she'd said he'd saved her from the evil clutches of her in-laws. That was what this was all about.

And if he was protecting her, then that must mean he cared about her. How much, was the question.

Her heart thumped, but she needed to take this one step at a time. "It's because you can't give me a baby, isn't it?"

He blanched, then nodded jerkily. "Yes."

"But I've already got a son," she said gently.

"You want more children. Hell, you deserve more."

That pulled her up and she frowned at him. "Why do you think I want more children?"

"I see you with Josh and the way you love him. I see what a wonderful mother you are. And I remember you said you wanted a big family one day."

She gasped, then quickly tried to reason with him. Or lose him. "Yes, I did say I wanted a big family. But I didn't say I *had* to have one."

His face turned stubborn. "It's no use talking about it, Vanessa. Nothing's going to change. I can't give you a baby. And you need more children to make you complete."

"No!" She hurried to stand in front of him and cupped his face with her hands, looking up at his chiseled jaw, his firm mouth and those blue eyes that hid compassion for others but accepted none for himself. "I love you, Kirk," she said, seeing something flare in his eyes. "I love you with all my heart. I'm not about to let you go. Not ever. I don't care about having another baby if I don't have you. You're enough for me. You're all I'll ever want."

His big body shuddered. "You don't know what you're saying."

"Listen to me. I…don't…care…about…having…another…baby," she repeated slowly, emphasizing each and every word.

"No!" He stepped back and put some distance between them.

She stood looking at him. He wasn't listening to her anymore. He wasn't about to change his mind.

And perhaps he had more than one reason?

A thought sucked the air from her lungs. "Do you love Samantha after all? Is that what this is really about?"

"No! I never loved her in the first place."

Thank God! Then for some reason she said, "I've never asked this question before but how do you know you didn't love her?"

He looked surprised. "I just know."

Out of the blue, understanding dawned. A knot loosened inside her. "Do you love me, Kirk?"

Their eyes met and she saw the shock run through him.

"No," he said on a rough whisper.

"Are you sure?" she persisted, fighting for their future together. Their life. He was as scared emotionally as she had been of loving and losing. She understood that feeling only too well.

He straightened, his face like rock. "As I said, this is about you, not me. I'd rather hate myself now, than have you hate me in years to come."

That would never happen.

"It's over, Vanessa."

She looked at him and knew she would never get the chance to find out anyway. He was the immovable brick wall—immovable because he thought he was doing the right thing. He thought he was rescuing her again, this time from herself.

She wouldn't get through to him now.

There was only one thing left to do.

She held out her arms. "Make love to me, Kirk. Make love to me one last time before I go. You owe me that at least."

Eleven

Kirk escorted Vanessa down the hallway toward her bedroom, her hand in his.

Her heart in his.

Forever.

He wasn't sure how she'd comprehended something he hadn't even known about himself, but she was right.

He did love her.

It was the reason he knew the difference between what he'd felt for Samantha and what he now felt for Vanessa. There was no comparison. Vanessa was the love of his life.

And he had to let her go.

He didn't have a choice.

Inside the room he pulled her close and stilled, absorbing the feel of her, letting her absorb him, conscious of how well the two of them fitted together.

Like man and wife.

He lowered his head and placed his lips against hers…

And paused again…

Just for a moment…

Just so time could stand still.

She quivered, the sweet softness of her mouth trembling against him, and a current of need spurted through his veins. He pulled her closer, deepening the kiss, more than hungry for her. She was the emotional thirst in his life. He needed her *not* like he needed food, but like he needed water.

To live.

He became aware of her hands pushing lightly against his chest. She broke off the kiss, loosening his hold on her.

"Stand there," she murmured, stepping back, out of his arms, out of reach.

In the moonlight, she began to remove her clothes in front of him. His blood pulsed as she kicked off her sandals then reached behind to the zipper of her dress. He went to help but she put up her hand, motioning for him to stay where he was.

The summery material slid from her shoulders to the floor, exposing matching bra and panties. She quickly stripped them off and stepped over them, looking so very alluring in her nudity. His heart hammered in his chest as she lay down on the bed and held her hands out to him.

He undressed and joined her on the bed, cupping her face with his hands and kissing her until he could kiss her no more, until he had to stop and take a breath. He'd never love her more than he did at this moment.

Never love her less.

This was where he wanted her to stay.

In his arms.

Near his heart.

He kissed his way along her delicate jawline, the column

of her throat, to her breasts, taking turns to fit the dusky pink nipples in his mouth.

She whimpered his name and gripped his shoulders, her head thrown back, holding him to her as if he was everything she'd ever need.

He drew an unsteady breath.

Then other soft curves beckoned him. His lips began exploring her silken belly, the slim line of her hips, his hand moving lower, his fingers touching her intimately. She opened her legs and the scent of woman—Vanessa—swirled around him.

The headiest invitation.

Wanting the beautiful moment to last, he went up on his knees and knelt at her feet, taking his time to caress her slim calves, her trim thighs.

Her limbs trembled as he kissed his way up to where she waited for him. She quivered when he at last buried his face in the blond curls covering her femininity.

His tongue claimed her.

Aaaah….Vanessa.

He knew her taste. He would always know her taste. This was what love was all about. Not just about sex, but about knowing another person as well as yourself, body and soul.

She moaned his name and clutched his head in her hands, one minute just holding him, the next running her fingers through his hair. With each stroke of his tongue he felt the tension building inside her, not slow but fast now. When she began to move her body in rhythm with his tongue, he knew the time was right.

He let her go over the edge.

Let her freefall into the safe harbor of his love.

And when she came up for air, he positioned himself above her. It almost killed him not to slip inside her, not to feel her close around him, but the moment was too profound to rush. If he did nothing else in his life, he had to have this moment.

Her eyelids fluttered open. She blinked as if coming from a long way off, then focused her gaze on him with such love that he had to swallow hard.

He *did* love her, he wished he could say to her out loud. No matter where she was, he would always love her. As if she could read his mind, her green eyes shimmered and he knew that at last she'd truly realized this was all they would have together.

Then she blinked back the tears and reached up to run the back of her fingers down his cheek. "I love you, my darling. I always will."

Their eyes locking on each other, he sank into her, joining their bodies together, their two hearts beating as one as he started the final part of the journey.

He began to move, back and forth, each thrust sending a wave of the deepest pleasure through him until the tension built and could go no further. He reached breaking point and she pulsed around him. A heartbeat later he freed his passion deep inside her.

And when he took another breath, he knew he'd said goodbye to the woman he loved.

The next morning it all came rushing back to Vanessa before she had even opened her eyes. She'd spent the night in Kirk's arms, each stroke, each touch revealing how much he loved her, no matter that he hadn't said the words out loud. It had been so beautiful, she'd cried afterward. They'd loved each other twice more after that, but both times had been fast and with a desperation that had made her eyes glisten.

Lifting her head from his chest now, she looked at him as he slept. His hair was tousled and a shadow of beard dusted his lean cheeks and chin. The muscled expanse of male chest sprinkled with dark curling hair had her barely resisting the urge to touch the warm ripple of flesh.

But if she did that she would wake him. And when he woke up she would have to pack her things and leave. She held back a sob. She didn't know if she could bear it.

He opened his eyes and she saw the exact moment he recalled the night…and the exact moment he remembered this day.

A mixture of tenderness and deep regret crossed his face, a regret that echoed in her heart. Goodbyes were never easy, but this goodbye made her feel as if she were dying inside.

He reached out and smoothed her hair. "What time is it?" he murmured.

"Six o'clock." She'd stop time if she could, she thought, her throat closing up, her body aching for more of his touch but now, more than ever, she had to be strong.

Just then, his cell phone rang from the direction of his trousers. They both froze, knowing this was the last time they would be together like this.

He threw the sheet aside. "The world intrudes," he muttered, sliding out of bed to pick up his trousers from the chair, gloriously naked, the line of his buttocks firm, his body so beautifully proportioned that her breath hitched in her throat.

Unable to look at him any longer, she closed her eyes, keeping the tears at bay. She didn't want him to remember her a soggy mess of emotion. She wanted him to remember her as a woman who picked herself up and got on with life. She wouldn't burden him with her love any more than she already had. It was the best, most honorable thing she could do for him.

There was a brief pause in movement and she felt him looking at her. Then he started to talk into the phone and she opened her eyes, hearing him say he'd be right there.

He ended the call. "That was one of the men. I'm needed down at the yards."

She nodded, understanding his need to go but selfishly not wanting this moment to end. It was too quick.

Would slower be any better?

No, it wouldn't.

He came over and gave her a hard kiss. "I'll be back later to take you into Jackaroo Plains," he said brusquely. "Can you be ready by eleven?"

She nodded, unable to speak.

He pulled away and strode to the door, but once there he stopped and looked back. Their eyes met one more time.

Once more with feeling.

Kirk spent most of the morning with his men sorting out the problem with one of the machines, then it was time to go back to the house. He drove with a heavy heart. It had almost killed him to turn his back on Vanessa's offer of a life together but he had to keep remembering it was for *her* sake he was doing this. He could not relent. It had to be goodbye.

Easier said than done when he saw her luggage stacked side-by-side inside the front door. The realness of her leaving shook him down to his boots. This place was going to be so empty without her and Josh.

He drew his shoulders back and continued down the hallway to find them. It was quieter than expected, as if they'd already gone.

Just then, he heard Suzi barking out the back of the house. An odd premonition trickled down his spine and uneasiness washed over him. Something was up.

Vanessa!

Josh!

He began to run through the house and was about to burst

through the back screen door when he saw her. He skidded to a halt and breathed a huge sigh of relief on seeing her standing near the shed door, holding a barking Suzi. Josh was nowhere in sight so was probably taking a nap.

Then he frowned. Vanessa was trying to stop the little dog from wriggling out of her arms. He went still as a cold flash rode down his spine.

A snake lay coiled on the ground across the yard from her. Large and brown and vicious. A King Brown. One of the deadliest snakes in the world who could inject a large quantity of venom with a single bite. Even as he watched, the snake's head rose, its fangs flashing in and out of its mouth as it sensed a presence.

"Vanessa," he muttered, terrified it would attack her. Yet if she let Suzi go, the little dog would race at the snake to protect her pups. Kirk knew that Vanessa wouldn't let Suzi get bitten and die.

But what about herself?

Fear squeezed the breath from his lungs as he looked around for a stick or a rake. Anything to stop the snake from striking the woman he loved. If it did, he knew there was little chance of her surviving. The thought of losing Vanessa was unfathomable and made the blood chill in his veins. He had to do something and do it now.

The rifle!

Silently and quickly he hurried to retrieve it from the gun cabinet, the metal smooth and familiar beneath his fingers as he took off the safety catch and prepared it for firing.

Suzi had momentarily stopped barking and the click of the rifle being cocked caught Vanessa's attention, but he didn't have time to think beyond the moment. Finding his target, he took aim and fired. His first shot hit but didn't kill and he rapidly cocked the rifle again. The injured snake was mad now and it reared its head up ready to strike Vanessa. Kirk fired. The snake's head exploded into thin air.

Putting the safety catch back on, he placed the rifle against the side of the house. For a moment he stood there trying not to shake, trying not to think about what could have happened just now.

Then he pulled himself together and strode toward her. Vanessa put Suzi on the ground and the small dog made a beeline for her pups inside the barn. Then with a small sob, Vanessa met him halfway and threw her arms around his neck.

He gathered her close. "You could have been killed," he muttered, hugging her tight, locking his hands on her back, holding her against him. He didn't want to let her go.

He *never* wanted to let her go again.

"Oh, Kirk, thank God you came along. And thank God Josh wasn't with me."

He pressed his lips against her neck, the living warmth of her skin a reminder of what he'd almost lost.

It hit him then that Vanessa had been right. It *didn't* matter that he couldn't give her a child. What mattered was that the two of them belonged together.

He pulled back to look down at her and love rose up in his throat, choking him and making it difficult for him to speak. "I love you, Vanessa," he said thickly. "More than life itself. I won't let you leave me. I'll never let you go. You and Josh." He showed his heart in his eyes. It was hers for the taking, and he gave her all of it.

"Oh, darling," she murmured, wondrous joy written on her face.

He crushed her to him and their lips met in a kiss that was beautiful in its intensity. It held the promise of the future, by conceding to the past. They had finally come to the place where they could be the best of themselves.

With each other.

Sparks of happiness leaping inside her, Vanessa finally made it up for air. This was where she belonged—in Kirk's arms—today and all the tomorrows they'd share.

"So what are we going to do about us?" she teased huskily.

His arms rested on her hips. "We're getting married. I'm not letting you out of my sight ever again. I love you, Vanessa. I would have died a slow death without you."

She melted at the look of love glowing from his very being. It encompassed her as a whole, acknowledged her as a woman, accepted her as an equal, and told her he'd placed his heart in her hands for safekeeping.

"You know," he said. "We could always try for adoption in a few years' time. What do you think?"

Her love bubbled over. "Oh, yes! I'd like that. I'd like that very much."

"Then we'll try, my love." He paused with a tilt to his head.

She frowned. "What are you doing?"

"Listening for Josh. He must have slept through the whole thing."

Her heart filled with tenderness. This was the way it would be from now on. Kirk would always look after her son and put him first when need be.

Their son.

"Yes, he's still sleeping," she said, showing him the small digital baby monitor she'd tucked into her jeans pocket.

Swinging her up in his arms, he started toward the house. "Good, because right now there's something I need to do."

"What's that?" She wrapped her arms around his neck, knowing by the dazzling light in his eyes what he would say.

"Make love to you," he murmured, then stopped to kiss her.

They only made it as far as the sunlit verandah before he

collapsed on the outdoor sofa and pulled her onto his lap. He kissed her again and his hand slid under her blouse to cup her breast, making her gasp and break off the kiss.

"Kirk, what if someone comes and catches us?" she said, more than a little breathless by now.

He smiled that sexy smile of his she knew would still turn her heart over in fifty years' time. "That's the beauty of the outback, darling. We have it all to ourselves."

She closed her eyes and let him have his way. She could easily get used to making love with the sun on her back.

And she did.

* * * * *

Don't miss the next book from
Maxine Sullivan
coming June 8, 2010
from Silhouette Desire.

*Harlequin Intrigue top author Delores Fossen presents
a brand-new series of breathtaking romantic suspense!*
TEXAS MATERNITY: HOSTAGES
*The first installment available May 2010:
THE BABY'S GUARDIAN*

Shaw cursed and hooked his arm around Sabrina.

Despite the urgency that the deadly gunfire created, he tried to be careful with her, and he took the brunt of the fall when he pulled her to the ground. His shoulder hit hard, but he held on tight to his gun so that it wouldn't be jarred from his hand.

Shaw didn't stop there. He crawled over Sabrina, sheltering her pregnant belly with his body, and he came up ready to return fire.

This was obviously a situation he'd wanted to avoid at all cost. He didn't want his baby in the middle of a fight with these armed fugitives, but when they fired that shot, they'd left him no choice. Now, the trick was to get Sabrina safely out of there.

"Get down," someone on the SWAT team yelled from the roof of the adjacent building.

Shaw did. He dropped lower, covering Sabrina as best he could.

There was another shot, but this one came from a rifleman on the SWAT team. Shaw didn't look up, but he heard the sound of glass being blown apart.

The shots continued, all coming from his men, which meant it might be time to try to get Sabrina to better cover. Shaw glanced at the front of the building.

So that Sabrina's pregnant belly wouldn't be smashed

against the ground, Shaw eased off her and moved her to a sitting position so that her back was against the brick wall. They were close. Too close. And face-to-face.

He found himself staring right into those sea-green eyes.

How will Shaw get Sabrina out?
Follow the daring rescue and the heartbreaking
aftermath in THE BABY'S GUARDIAN by Delores Fossen,
available May 2010 from Harlequin Intrigue.

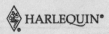
HARLEQUIN®

INTRIGUE

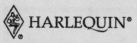
HARLEQUIN®

LAURA MARIE ALTOM

The Baby Twins

Stephanie Olmstead has her hands full raising
her twin baby girls on her own. When she runs
into old friend Brady Flynn, she's shocked to find
herself suddenly attracted to the handsome airline
pilot! Will this flyboy be the perfect daddy—
or will he crash and burn?

Babies
&
Bachelors
USA

"LOVE, HOME & HAPPINESS"

www.eHarlequin.com

HAR75309

Former bad boy Sloan Hawkins is back in
Redemption, Oklahoma, to help keep his aunt's
cherished garden thriving and to reconnect with the
girl he left behind, Annie Markham. But when he
discovers his secret child—and that single mother
Annie never stopped loving him—he's determined
that a wedding will take place in the garden
nurtured by faith and love.

Where healing flows...

Look for

The Wedding Garden
by Linda Goodnight

*Available May 2010
wherever you buy books.*

Steeple
Hill®
LI87595

www.SteepleHill.com

HARLEQUIN
Ambassadors

Want to share your passion for reading Harlequin® Books?

Become a Harlequin Ambassador!

Harlequin Ambassadors are a group of passionate and well-connected readers who are willing to share their joy of reading Harlequin® books with family and friends.

You'll be sent all the tools you need to spark great conversation, including free books!

All we ask is that you share the romance with your friends and family!

You'll also be invited to have a say in new book ideas and exchange opinions with women just like you!

To see if you qualify* to be a Harlequin Ambassador, please visit www.HarlequinAmbassadors.com.

*Please note that not everyone who applies to be a Harlequin Ambassador will qualify. For more information please visit www.HarlequinAmbassadors.com.

Thank you for your participation.

BAP09BPA

REQUEST YOUR FREE BOOKS!

2 FREE NOVELS
PLUS 2
FREE GIFTS!

Passionate, Powerful, Provocative!

HARLEQUIN® *Blaze*™

is proud to present

***New York Times* bestselling author**

Vicki Lewis Thompson

with a brand-new trilogy,
SONS OF CHANCE
where three sexy brothers
meet three irresistible women.

Look for the first book
WANTED!

Available beginning in June 2010
wherever books are sold.

---

red-hot reads

www.eHarlequin.com

HB79548